melville house classics

THE
ENCHANTED
WANDERER

THE ENCHANTED WANDERER

NIKOLAI LESKOV

TRANSLATED BY IAN DREIBLATT

MELVILLE HOUSE
BROOKLYN · LONDON

THE ENCHANTED WANDERER BY NIKOLAI LESKOV
WAS FIRST SERIALIZED IN *RUSSKIY MIR*, ST. PETERSBURG, IN 1873

© 2012 MELVILLE HOUSE
TRANSLATION © 2012 IAN DREIBLATT

FIRST MELVILLE HOUSE PRINTING: AUGUST 2012

MELVILLE HOUSE PUBLISHING
145 PLYMOUTH STREET
BROOKLYN, NY 11201

WWW.MHPBOOKS.COM

ISBN: 978-1-61219-103-4

BOOK DESIGN: CHRISTOPHER KING, BASED ON
A SERIES DESIGN BY DAVID KONOPKA

MANUFACTURED IN THE UNITED STATES OF AMERICA

1 2 3 4 5 6 7 8 9 10

  LIBRARY OF CONGRESS CONTROL NUMBER: 2012945586

THE ENCHANTED WANDERER

I

We sailed across Lake Ladoga from Konevets Island to Valaam, stopping by Korela Harbor for maintenance. A wanderlust washed over the ship, and we rode some little Finnish horses into the desolate village and back. It was not long before the captain had finished his business, and we set off again.

After the stopover in Korela, it was only natural that our talk turned to that poor – though venerable – Holyrussian village, than which it is hard to imagine anyplace more desolate. Everyone on board was of one mind about it, and one of us, a man disposed to philosophical prattle and political pretensions, told us all about how he had never for the life of him understood why the authorities off in Petersburg saw fit year after year to send undesirables to far-off regions, more or less remote, and always at public expense, when just east of the capital there was Lake Ladoga, dotted with little ports like Korela, where no free thought and no *joie de vivre* could possibly survive the ignorance of the locals and the horrendously dull local landscape.

"I am quite certain," he declared, "that the situation can be blamed on bureaucratic inertia, or, if nothing else, a lack of thorough investigation."

Someone else, a regular traveler through the area, answered that it had at various times been home to outcasts of all sorts, but had failed to hold any of them for long.

"One young man, a seminarian, was sent off here as punishment," he told us, "for a discourtesy he had shown as a deacon (a punishment I've never been able to understand). After arriving, he bore up reasonably well, strengthened by the hope that his fortunes would soon turn up; but then he took to drink, and drank and drank until finally he'd been driven fully out of his mind and filed a formal petition that he 'be shot, or conscripted into the army, or hanged for general incapacity.'"

"Well, what was the decision?"

"Well, in truth there's... no way to say. You see, he didn't wait for any kind of a response: he hanged himself on his own authority."

"I'd say he resolved things beautifully!" the philosopher responded.

"Beautifully?" asked the storyteller, a merchant by the look of him, sober and religious.

"Why not? At least he put his miseries to an end."

"An end to his miseries? Fine thought! And what of his soul, in the next life? You know, there are whole centuries of special torment lying in wait for suicides. It is even forbidden the living to pray for them!"

The philosopher grinned venomously and said nothing.

But then a new voice entered the fray, taking neither side. Surprisingly, this man took the position that the deacon had executed justice on his own, and merely spared the authorities the burden of his case.

This was a new passenger; none of us had noticed him embarking at Konevets. He had been silent until this, no one paying him any mind, but now we all turned to him in shared wonderment: how had such a man possibly gone among us till now without comment? He was, for one thing, enormously tall, with darkish skin, an openness in his expression, and thick, curly hair the color of lead, a graying mane that poured forth in a terribly strange way. He was dressed in a short cassock, with the wide leather belt of a monk, and, in black cotton, a high ecclesiastical hat. He might have been a novice or tonsured in an order – it was impossible to say, because the monks around Lake Ladoga do not always wear skullcaps when they travel, or even when going about their business on the islands; instead, in their rustic simplicity, they often limit themselves to these tall ecclesiastical hats. Our new passenger, a man we would soon be fascinated by, seemed at least fifty; and from the looks of him, he was in every sense a bogatyr, and at that a humble, kindly Russian bogatyr, the sort one might imagine, recalling Ilya Muromets as he appears in Vereshchagin's masterly painting, or is limned in the poetry of Count Alexei Tolstoy. It seemed he would be at home not traipsing around in a cassock but rather sitting on the "dappled steed" of an adventure story, thundering through a wood in jute shoes, and taking in "the scents of the sap and the strawberries wafting through the pine."

But for all his unassuming good nature, one did not have to look too closely to see that he, as they say, had *been around*. He carried himself bravely, possessed self-assurance without any vain swagger, and when he spoke out it was in warm, well-practiced bass:

"Doesn't mean a thing," he began, letting one word after another drip softly, lazily, from under his thick, gray mustache, which curled upward after the Hussar fashion. "I don't agree with you about suicides, saying they can never be forgiven. And as for there being no one to pray for them – well, that's rubbish too, because I know someone who, very simply, can set their situation to right, with the lightest touch."

We asked him, who was this man, who settled the affairs of suicides already dead?

"The man you're asking about," the Hero in Black began, "is a little priestling in a little village near Moscow. A terrible drunk, almost defrocked even – he works it out for them."

"And how did you come to know about it?"

"My goodness, gentlemen – it's not just me who knows about it, but everyone in the Moscow diocese. Especially since the involvement of His High Excellency, Metropolitan Filaret."

There was a brief quiet, and then someone pointed out how fishy it all sounded.

The Black Cassock answered, without a hint of offense:

"Oh, sure, at first glance it's a little doubtful. And we shouldn't be surprised – even His High Excellency didn't believe it for a long time. Finally, seeing the evidence, he realized there was no way *not* to believe it. Had to be true."

The passengers began to dog the monk to tell them the whole, wondrous story, and he didn't refuse. It went like this:

Well, it seems that one day a deacon wrote to His Eminence the bishop, to say, well, so-and-so, that little priest out there? He's an outrageous drunk, swilling wine constantly, a black mark on the parish. Truth be told, this wasn't unjustified. The bishop sent for the little priest to appear before him in Moscow. When they got a look at him, it was plain as day – priestling was a real sot, and they decided to strip him of his appointment. The little priest was devastated, even stopped drinking, went soft and would weep constantly. 'Oh what have I come to!' he thought. 'Is there anything left for me but to do myself in? That's it – at least then the bishop will take pity on my poor family and marry off my daughters, find someone who can take my place and keep bread on the table.' So he'd decided to do himself in, and then the appointed day finally dawned and he thought to himself – he'd always been a gentle spirit – *Okay, let's say, I die. I'm not an animal, not without a soul – what's to become of my immortal soul, after I do this?* And then he began to stew about it. He stewed and stewed, and meanwhile the bishop – the one who had stripped him of his position – he lay down on the couch with a book after a big meal one day and drifted off to sleep. Drifted off or passed out, but no sooner is His Eminence sawing wood than the door to his cell starts opening. He shouts, 'Who's there?' thinking it's probably his assistant come to tell him of a visitor. No, not the assistant: in walks an old man, on his face a kindness beyond kindness, and His Grace recognizes him immediately as the Right Reverend Sergius!

The bishop says, "Can it be you, Holy Father Sergius?"

And the holyman answers, "It is, Filaret, ye servant of God."

The bishop asks, "What could it be that you, Immaculate One, desire of me, unworthy as I am?"

And Saint Sergius answers: "It's mercy that I want."

"And to whom would you have me show it?"

And so the saint named that little priest, the drunk everyone had forgotten. And then the bishop woke up, and thought to himself, *What's it all driving at? An ordinary dream, or one that took a flight of fancy, or a vision sent by spirits?* And he began to mull it over, a man known the world around for his intellect, and finally decided on ordinary dream – after all, how likely was it that Saint Sergius, famous for his fasting, for the good and strict life he led, would come around for that weak soul, like a field overgrown with weeds? Having worked this out, His Eminence resolved to leave the whole business to its natural conclusion, as he'd been planning at first, and when his bedtime rolled around, he went off to sleep as usual. But no sooner had he laid him down than another vision came, and it terrified him. Just you picture this: a thundering... oh, such a terrible thundering that there's no way to describe it… Then, a galloping… horsemen beyond number… they surge in green chain mail, breastplates, feathers, the warhorses like so many lions, like ravens, and in front of them their proud commander, dressed the same, and wherever he waves his dark standard, they surge, and on the standard a serpent. The bishop doesn't know what's happening, and just then the captain roars out an order: "Slice them to pieces: there's no prayers for them!" And he gallops off. And behind the captain fly his soldiers, and after them, a procession of weary shades walks by like a skinny flock of springtime geese, nodding at His Grace one by one, crying pitifully, entreating him softly between sobs, "Let him go! He's the only one who prays for us." As soon as he wakes up, the bishop calls for the drunken little priest and starts peppering him with questions: How does he pray, and for whom? And the priest, as weak a spirit as ever, was flummoxed by the great man's presence, and could only say: "Your Grace, I perfect my duties exactly as prescribed." It took great force to drag the truth out of him. "I'm guilty of one sin," he said. "Being weak in spirit myself, and having once been driven by despair to make designs on my own life, at Holy Mass each week I say an extra prayer for those who die by their own hands in want of absolution…" The bishop understood at once who those shades had been that drifted before him like skinny geese in his vision, and, not wanting to make those murderous demons glad, he gave the little priest his blessing. "Go on," he said, "but in fear of sin no longer. And whoever you were praying for, pray for them still." And the priestling was restored to his former office, always around to lend a hand to those who find life too burdensome to go on, unshaking in his duty. And he will always hassle his Creator on their behalf, Who will be required to forgive them.

"What do you mean, *required*?"

"Because, 'Knock and it shall be opened.' That's the word of the Lord Himself, and that cannot be changed."

"Well, tell us, please, is there anyone else who prays for suicides, beside that Moscow priest?"

"Well now, I really don't know quite what to say to that. They say you mustn't pray God for them, that they follow their own law instead of His, but I bet that some people misunderstand this and pray for them anyway. And there's one day, I think it's on Trinity Sunday, or maybe Pentecost Monday, when everyone's allowed to pray for them. And what special prayers they read that day! Miraculous prayers, soul-melting – I could listen to them forever."

"And you're not allowed to read them other days?"

"I wouldn't know. Only an educated man would know. And as for me – I'm not interested. I've never debated it with anyone."

"But have you ever noticed hearing those prayers repeated at services?"

"No, I haven't, but don't take my word for it – I rarely make it to church."

"Well, why's that?'

"I'm very busy. I don't have the time."

"Well, are you a hieromonk? A hierodeacon?"

"No, for now I'm just wearing this monk's habit."

"But that must mean you're a monk of some kind, yes?"

"Well… yes. At least, I tend to be seen as one."

"You're seen however you're seen," the merchant replied to this, "but I've seen men in monks' habits thrown into the army!"

The bogatyr in the Black Cassock gave no sign of offense at all. He just sat in thought for a minute and then said, "Yes, I think it could probably happen, or at least people say it does. Except that I'm pretty old already, fifty-three now, and besides no stranger to army life."

"You served in the armed forces?'

"I did."

"Well, then you must have been a non-commissioned officer, I presume?" the merchant asked.

"No, not a non-commissioned officer."

"So what were you? A watchman, a quartermaster, what? Animal, vegetable, or mineral?"

"No, it's not like that at all. I was a true military man; I've been involved in regimental affairs almost since I was a little boy."

"Okay then, you must be a cantonist?" the merchant said, really starting to heat up.

"Not that either."

"Well alright, the devil take you! Who are you already?"

"I'm a *connoisseur*."

"A whaa-aat?"

"I'm a connoisseur. You might just say I'm smart with horses. Army officers had me on, acting as their advisor."

"Well, that's something!"

"I won't say it isn't – I've chosen and broken at least a few thousand. Why, I've trained wild ones that used to rear up and fall back, crushing the rider under the saddlebow. Oh, they kicked, sure, but none of them could throw me."

"How would you deal with those?"

"For me it's always been easy. I was born with a feeling for horses. Why, I'd no sooner mount one than I'd grip his left ear and yank it with all my strength, while landing a blow with my right fist right between his ears – all faster than the poor beast had a chance to get his bearings – and I'd grind my teeth awfully, and such a gush from his nostrils that you'd look for brains in it. That calms 'em down, boy."

"Well, alright, but after that?"

"After that, you hop off, look him over, let him look *you* over so he gets a good impression, one that'll last, and then you hop back on and ride him away."

"And the horse becomes obedient, after this?"

"Oh, sir, it breaks him! You see, a horse is a clever animal; he can tell what kind of a man he's dealing with. In my case, every horse I've ridden loved me and feared me. I remember one courser at an equestrian school in Moscow that was throwing off every rider that tried him. The fiend had even learned a trick where he bit through a rider's knee – right to the marrow! This devil would just get his huge teeth around the kneecap and chomp right in! He'd caused a lot of deaths. Around that time an Englishman by the name of Rarey – they called him "the Wild Tamer" – came to Moscow, and this hangdog mongrel beast gave him no small bite! Shamed him completely. They say he only got away with his life because he wore a steel kneeguard, so the blasted thing couldn't bite through and tossed him off instead. But for that, another victim would've fallen to the creature. But I taught him some manners."

"Well, please, friend, tell us how you did it!"

"I did it through God's will, because, I'll remind you, I have a divine gift for it. This Mister Rarey, this so called Wild Tamer, and all the others who'd tried to break him, they all thought in conquering the courser's temper the trick would be to hold on to the reins so that he couldn't move that watermelon of a head to either side! So just as soon as Rarey declared he'd have nothing more to do with the thing, then I say, 'Oh, what a fuss." I say, "there's nothing to it! He's a fine steed, he's just got the devil in his spirit. This Brit doesn't get it, but I do – let me help." The academy's directors agreed at once. So then I said, "Take him out behind the Drogomilovsky guardpost!" They took him. We led him by the bridle to a hollow in the Fillies, where the gentry have their summer dachas. And right away I see: here's a spacious, comfortable place, let's get going. I jump right on him, that man-eater, bare-chested, no shoes, nothing but a pair of wide britches and a cap. And twisted around my naked torso a braided cotton cincture, consecrated to the brave and holy Prince Vsevolod-Gabriel of Novgorod, trusted protector, doer of great deeds, whom I've admired since my youth, and emblazoned on it the motto: *My honor I shall surrender to none.* No special tools, except in one hand a strong Tatar whip with a lead handle, no more than two pounds altogether, and, in the other, an ordinary crock of thin dough. While I was sitting up there, four different attendants pulled on his muzzle in four different directions, to keep those awful teeth from gnashing into any of them. And he, that monstrous horse, he begins to see that we're turning the tables on him, he starts neighing and squealing and breaking a sweat, writhing in fury, I can see he wants to gobble me whole. So I shout to the stableman, "Hurry up," I tell him, "unbridle the demon!" Well, they couldn't believe their ears, never expected me to say such a thing! And they just stood there, giving me the hairy eyeball.

So then I say, Well what are you standing around for! Can't you hear me? Do as I tell you, immediately! But they responded, "What's got into you, Ivan Severyanych – my name in the world used to be Ivan Severyanych, or more formally Flyagin – how is it even possible, they asked, that you want us to take off the bridle!?" I began to get really angry with them, because I could sense and even feel with my legs that that horse was going feral with rage, so I dug into him real good with my knees and I shrieked the order again, "Take it off!" They had something else to say, but now I really lost it and ground my teeth together till they squealed, so that they finally yanked the bridle off and scattered like mad in every direction. Well, as soon as it was off I became the first one to give that vile horse a real surprise: smashed that crock right into the crown of his head, smashed it and shattered it so the dough dripped down all over his eyes and up into his nostrils. Now he got scared: "What's going on here?!" But before he could even think I took my cap off and began rubbing the dough into his eyes with it, while with my other hand I smashed the whip across his right side. Oh boy, did he give a run! I keep on rubbing the dough in his eyes and bringing that whip down on him, and we ride on and on and I show him no mercy, not a second to breathe, keeping his eyes blocked, the whip crashing down over him, first one side then the other, making sure he got the message that I wasn't messing around… And understand it he did, as you could tell, because he didn't linger in one place for a second, but kept charging off for all he was worth! He bore me on and on, the pitiful beast, bore me while I thrashed and thrashed him, and the faster he charged the more ferociously I beat him, until finally we both began to get tired: my shoulder started aching and my arm was too fatigued to raise the whip, while he had stopped looking around and his tongue was hanging out. I could see he was ready to give, so I jumped down, wiped off his eyes, grabbed him by a tuft of mane, and said, "Is that enough for you, you rotten lump of meat, you monster?!" And I yanked his hair so hard that he collapsed onto his knees in front of me, and from that day forward he was such a lamb. You couldn't ask for a tamer animal: he'd let anyone mount and ride him. Only he wasn't long for this world."

"Kicked the bucket, eh?"

"You might say so. Such a proud creature, and even if forced to be gentle, it seems his spirit couldn't surrender. And that gentleman Rarey, when he heard the whole story, immediately invited me to come work for him."

"And did you?'

"No."

"How come?"

"Oh, what can I tell you! First of all, because I'm a connoisseur, and more accustomed to that end of things – to choosing horses, I mean, rather than breaking them in, which had to be what it was he wanted from me, and second of all, because, for all I knew, he was really planning to get the better of me somehow."

"Get the better of you? How do you mean?"

"He wanted me to turn over my secret."

"But would you have given it to him?"

"Oh, I would have, for a price."

"So what got in the way of things?"

"Well… it must have been when he became afraid of me."

"Afraid of you? You can't stop now – tell us the story behind that."

"Nothing to tell, really. One day he just said to me, 'Tell me your secret, brother, I'll pay well for it and hire you as my connoisseur.' But since it's just not in me to swindle anyone, all I could think to say was, 'What secret? Don't be silly.' But he was a typical Englishman, thinking everything a point to be learned, and he didn't believe me. So then he says, 'If you won't open up to me now, let's have a spot of rum together!' So the two of us drank rum till his face went red and, doing his best, he said, 'Come on now, out with it – tell me what you did to that courser!'"

So I answer, "Alright, here's what…" and flash him the

evilest look I can, and I start grinding my teeth, and since I don't have a crock of dough I grab a glass from the table and fake like I'm going to smash him with it – this is just for a demonstration, mind you – but no sooner does he get a look at it all than he dives under the table and bolts for the door. That's the last time I saw him. He's never crossed my path again."

"And that's why you didn't end up with the job?"

"That's why. I mean, how could I even tell him I wanted the job if he was too afraid to meet up with me? Now, understand – I would've loved to run into him somewhere. I really got to like him during our little rum-drinking contest. But you know how it is, you can't outrun destiny, and my path was leading another way…"

"So, did you find a calling for yourself?"

"I'm afraid that I don't quite know how to put it… I've traveled all over, I've ridden on horses and under them, I've been a prisoner and a soldier, beaten other men and been beaten by them, sometimes so badly that I barely survived."

"And when did you take your vows at the monastery?"

"Just recently, only a few years after all these adventures ended."

"And I suppose you must have felt you'd found your true calling then?"

"Well, um, I… I don't know how to explain it. But then, it seems that I must have."

"Why do you say it like that? How can you be so unsure about it?"

"I can't speak surely about it any more than I can embrace having my own vitality sapped."

"Sapped? By what?"

"By the other men whose wills I acted on, rather than my own."

"What? Whose?"

"It all goes back to a vow made by my mother and father."

"A vow? What kind of vow?"

"A vow that I would live all my life on the very brink of death, and never actually manage to die."

"Is that so?"

"It's exactly so, sir."

"Well then, please sir, tell us the story of your life."

"Alright, but the only thing is, I can only remember it all if I start from my very earliest beginnings. If you'll indulge me…"

"Certainly – tell us everything. That'll be more interesting, anyway."

"I'm afraid I can't say much for how interesting it'll be, but kindly listen in and I'll tell you everything."

II

Here is how the former connoisseur Ivan Severyanych –
this Mister Flyagin – began his tale:

I was born a serf among the people of Count K, of the
Orlovsky Region. The titles to these lands must have been
divided by now among the younger gentry, but in the old
Count's day they were considerable. In the little town of G,
where the Count himself had chosen to live, he had a colos-
sal, rich mansion, with a little annex on it for guests, its own
theater, a special bowling alley, a kennel, a whole menagerie
of live bears, gardens, his own choir to give concerts, his
own actors to stage scenes for him, even his own textile
workshops, with workers skilled enough to make the most
esoteric patterns; but more than anything else, it was his
stud farm that captured his attentions. Each division had
its own people allocated to run it, and the stables always got
the most attention – just like army conscripts who know
their sons'll be cantonists, a driver knew his boy'd grow to
be a driver, every stableman's son a stableboy looking after

horses, and if you're the poor guy lugging fodder up from the thresher to the stalls, well, your boy's a little fodderer too then. My father was Severyan, a driver, and though he wasn't one of the head coachmen – we had a great many – he still drove a carriage-and-six, and once on a visit from the Tsar he rode in the seventh rank and was presented with a navy-blue bank note, an ancient one. As for my mother – I was born an orphan, as it were, since I was my mother's *prayer-son*. Barren a long time, she had prayed and pestered God so badly that finally, after many years, she died bringing me into this world, died bearing this big old head of mine, and that's also why no one ever called me Flyagin, but instead just "The Head." Living alongside my old father in the coachmen's quarters, I took to the mysteries of this great animal; you might even say that I became a lover of horses. As a baby I'd crawled around between their feet, and by the time I'd grown to a man I knew everything there was to know about a horse. The stud farm was its own world, the stables too, and we groomsmen didn't worry ourselves about the stud farm – just got horses from them, and broke them. Each driver and his outrider had six horses, all of different breeds: Vyatka horses, Kazan horses, Kalmyks, Bityugans, Don purebreds – all of these picked up at various fairs. Most of our horses, of course, came from the stud farm, but it hardly makes sense to talk about those: horses off stud farms are always weak in character and spirit, without the joyful mischief of dreams. These wild ones, though? Pure animals. The Count used to buy them, a whole drove at a time, at a great price, eight rubles a head, or maybe ten, and just as soon as we'd get them home he'd start training them. They resisted horribly! Some of 'em chose death over submitting. Half of 'em, sometimes. You'd see them out in the yard, shying away from even the walls, eyes slicing the sky like birds. Can't help pitying 'em, when you see them like that, aching, desperate for a pair of wings to fly away on… then they can't lower themselves to slop oats and water from a trough, and they start wasting away, wasting away, till they split in two. Yes, sometimes this was the fate of half the horses we bought, especially when we bought Kirghiz ones. They miss the freedom of the steppe. But of the horses who did submit, more than a few got maimed badly during their training. There's only one way to train a horse, and that's strictly. But the ones who made it through the training! Oh, such splendid beasts! No factory stud could ever compare.

My old father, Severyan Ivanych, drove a carriage with six Kirghiz horses, and when I grew up I started sitting as his outrider. The horses were cruel, not like those lambs you see cavalry officers trotting around on today. "Little courtiers" we used to call them, since there was no pleasure in riding something even an officer could ride; but my father's horses, these were monsters, vipers, basilisks, all in one: just a glance into their eyes, teeth, manes, flanks, was enough to terrify you. They knew no fatigue; you could drive them eighty versts, or a hundred, a hundred and fifteen versts from the manor all the way out to Oryol and back again, without a break, to these horses it was nothing. Once they got going, if you so much as blinked they'd leave you in the dust. Now when I first started outriding I was just eleven, and I had just the kind of voice that you'd expect, in those days, from the outrider of a nobleman: piercing and shrill, and so powerful I could shout *dititiooo* at the top of my lungs and drag out it for a half an hour. But I wasn't strong enough to keep myself in the saddle for long, and so on journeys I'd have them tie me to the horse – that is, to the saddle and the girth, and bind everything snugly, so that I couldn't possibly fall out. I'd be getting smashed to death, and more than once I lost feeling and went limp, but the bracing held me upright on the saddle, and after a while I got a good bump and came to. It happened like that more than once on the road – you pass out, you wake up – and afterward they'd have to crane me out of the saddle like a corpse, and then fetch some horseradish from the garden to stick under my nose and wake me; but after a while I got used to it, and I could take anything in stride. Sometimes you ride along just hoping you'll see a peasant so you can tear his shirt off with your whip as you pass – this is an old pastime of outriders.

One time we were driving the Count for a visit. It was a gorgeous summer day, and the Count was sitting with his dog in the open carriage, my poppa driving the four horses, me streaking up in front. We had to get off the turnpike at a crossroads and spend fifteen versts on the road to the P. Hermitage. It was a little roadway the monks had built, to make their monastery more inviting. It made fine sense – the highway was overgrown and wrecked, trees poking out at grotesque angles like knobby canes, while the monks' little road was clean and tidy, with a wall of hand-planted birches on either side, and those trees of such a shade and a fragrance, their road opening in the distance into an expanse of huge fields. In a word, it was beautiful, and I wanted to cry out – which was forbidden, of course, without good reason. So I kept it together, galloping along; but just then, three or four versts short of the monastery gate, I suddenly took a plunge, and right ahead of me I saw a little black spot... something walking along the road, like a little hedgehog. Well, this really got me going, and I called out as loud as I could *didititiooo*, and I shouted it for a whole verst until finally I overcame a farm cart pulled by two horses, that's who I'd been yelling at, and I stood myself up in the stirrups so I could see that someone was lying asleep on some hay in the wagon. There he lay, in another world, the sun warming him, peaceful as anything, the sleep so heavy on him, face down with his hands splayed out on either side, like he was trying to give the cart a big hug. But when I see he's not yielding, I pull over to one side of the road, and then, once I overtake him, standing in the reins, I start grinding my teeth and bring that whip down across his back with a terrible smack. The horses just bolted down the hillside, and the old man gave an awful start, wearing just the kind of ecclesiastical hat I've got on now, his face, oh just so *pitiful*, like some old hag's, and with such a fright come over it that he was weeping, and starting to flail around in the hay, like a gudgeon in a pan, and then reaching around for the edge of the hay – he was still half-asleep – he misjudged and tumbled out, mangling himself under the cartwheel, and his feet got tangled in the reins, dragging him along through the dust… At first I and my old man, and even the Count himself, thought it was pretty funny, how the old man had somersaulted along. But now I looked down and saw that the cart had been snagged on a branch just short of a bridge at the bottom of the hill, but the old monk didn't stand or stir. When we rode up a little closer, I saw that he was all covered in gray, and of his face not even the nose was left – just a horrible gash and blood pouring out of it. The Count had us stop, stepped out, looked him over, and said, "Dead." He said he should have me whipped and ordered that I hurry to the monastery. From there, some people were sent to the bridge, and the Count had a conversation with the Father Superior, and throughout the fall a parade of gifts was sent off to the monastery: a load of oats, then one of flour, then dried carp, and when we got to the monastery my father took me out behind the shed and gave me a whipping. It wasn't a terrible beating, though, because I had my duties and needed to get right back in the saddle again. And that was the end of it, except that that night the monk appeared to me in a dream, that one I'd throttled to death, and again, like a sad old woman, he was crying. So I say, "What do you want from me? Get lost!"

And then *he* says, "You," he says, "you did me in without a chance at repentance!"

"That's a tough break," I answer, "but what can I do about it now? You know I didn't do it on purpose. Besides," I say, "what've *you* got to complain about. You're dead now, and that's that!"

"Obviously," he says, "that's where we stand. And I'm very grateful to you for that – but I've come now from talking with your own true mother, to ask if you know that you're her *prayer son*?"

"What is this," I say. "I've heard that so many times, from my grandmother Fedosya, she brings it up constantly."

"Do you also know," he says, "that you're a *promised son*?"

"How do you mean?"

"I mean," he said, "that you've been promised. To God."

"And who promised me to Him?"

"Your mother."

"And why doesn't she come tell me herself? How do I know it's not just something you made up?"

"No," he said, "I didn't make it up. It's just that it's impossible for her to come here."

"Why's that?"

"Because," he says, "it's different for us here than it is for you on earth. Not everyone here talks, not everyone here can be seen, but when someone here is given the power to do something, he does it. And if you want," he goes on, "I'll give you a sign that my message is real."

"I *do* want," I tell him. "Only – what kind of sign?"

"The sign," he answers, "is that you'll live all your life on the very brink of death, and never actually manage to die, until the day appointed you finally dawns, and then you'll remember the promise of your mother and become a monk."

"Wonderful," I reply. "I'll await that day."

Then he disappeared, and I woke up and forgot all about it, never suspecting that all those troubles would arise and start befalling me one after the other. But just a short while later we were riding to Voronezh with the Count and Countess (they were taking their little daughter to the newly uncovered remains of a saint to cure her club-feet) and we stopped over to feed the horses in the Yeletsky Province, in the village of Krutoy. I dozed off under the deck, and who do I see – that little monk is back, the one I did in!

He says, "Listen, Head: I feel sorry for you. Ask your master for leave to become a monk; he'll grant it."

I answer, "Why in the world should I?"

And he responds, "Many are the evils that will befall you if you don't."

I think, I already killed you, may as well let you hem and haw at me, and then, getting up from all this, I helped my father ease the horses back to their harnesses, and we took off again, the road twisting and snaking through the mountains, on one side sheer cliffs that echoed with all the lives they'd claimed.

"Careful, Head, take it a little easier!" the Count called out.

But I was good in a spot like this. Even though it was the driver's job to hold the shaft horses' reins, I knew a lot of ways of helping my father. His shaft horses were strong and reliable; they had a way of easing the cart down an incline by sitting on their tails in the middle of the road. But one of them was a real blackguard, disposed to astronomy: just rein him in for a minute and he'd throw his head back, and, well bless his soul, cast his gaze to the heavens like he was scanning the stars! These astronomers! Basically, there's nothing worse, and especially between the drawbars, that's where they're most dangerous. An outrider's got to keep a close eye on an astronomer horse: on their own they can barely put one foot in front of the other, and they're always causing all kinds of problems. All this, of course, I knew about our astronomer, and I always tried to lend my father a hand: I'd grab the horse's reins next to mine in the crook of my left elbow and bring him down to steady him; then I'd push them so their tails pressed into the shaft horses' muzzles, with the shafts between their cruppers, and meantime I'd keep the whip right where that astronomer could see it, and if he began banking up into the clouds, *thwack*, right across the muzzle, and he'd keep his head down after that, so that the carriage would make it down the hill just fine. That's how it started this time: I was watching that astronomer, wiggling in the saddle to keep a good angle against him, and keeping him steady with the whip. And then I see that he's not responding to my father holding the reins, or even to my thrashings, and I could see his mouth dripping with blood from the bit and his eyes were rolled up in his head, and then I hear something crack behind me and, smack, the whole carriage starts barreling down the hill out of control. The break had snapped. I shout to my father, "Hold on! Hold on!" And he shouts back, "Hold on! Hold on!" But there was nothing left to hold onto – all six horses had broken into a mad rush down the hill, running every which way, and I see a flash through the air, my father, thrown from the cart – the reins had broken! And that terrible cliff right before us! I wish I could say whether it was for the masters or myself that I felt so afraid, but, at any rate, seeing the writing on the wall, I jumped up and got the shafts in my teeth and held on to them... I don't know what I weighed then, but in effect it must have been much more from all the force. So there I was, dangling. I pulled the necks of the draft horses in tight, so tight that it rattled in their throats when they breathed, and finally I marshaled the courage to open my eyes. The front horses were just gone, as though clipped cleanly from the front of the carriage, and I was dangling over the edge, the carriage standing behind me against the backs of the shaft horses I had nearly strangled.

It was only then that I had a chance to wake up to my fear, and my hands suddenly gave way and I flew down and can remember nothing further. I can't say how long I was out, but when I came to I was in some kind of an izba, and a burly peasant said, "Well, what's the word, little guy? You alive?"

"I suppose," I answered.

"And can you remember what happened to you?"

I started to remember and told him about how the horses had darted off and how I had ended up dangling over the cliff – but after that, I couldn't recall a thing.

"Right, how could you know what happened to you next?" he says. "But those horses of yours, they didn't get to the bottom in one piece, not by a damn sight. You only survived 'cause you landed on a lump of clay, and started sort of sledding down. We all thought you were a goner, but then we noticed you breathing. Figured you'd just got overwhelmed by all the rushing air. So," he went on, "get up now, stand up if you can, go quickly to see the saint. The Count left some money, said to bury you if you die, or send you to see him in Voronezh if you make it."

So I went. I didn't say a word the whole ride to Voronezh, just sat while this country idiot played barynyas on his accordion the whole way, wanting to throttle him.

As soon as I arrived in Voronezh, the Count had me sent for, and called me into his room, where he said to the Countess, "It seems we owe our lives to this young boy."

The Countess just nodded her head, and the Count added, "Tell me, Head, what do you want? I'll give you anything."

So I say, "I don't know what to ask for!"

And he says, "Well, what is it that you want?"

I thought and thought. Finally, I said, "An accordion."

The count laughed and replied, "True to God, you're an idiot, but no matter. I'll remember you, when the time comes. And meanwhile, you can have your accordion right away!"

One of the footmen went into town, and came back with an accordion, which he brought to me in the stables.

"Here you go," he said. "Play it."

I took it and tried to play, but soon figured out that I didn't know how. So I smashed it and tossed it away, and later some old hags on a religious quest fished it from under the stables and stole it.

When all of this happened, I should have pressed on the Count's kindness to be granted leave to a monastery, as the monk had advised me. I couldn't myself say why I'd asked for this accordion instead, running from my true calling so that one travesty after another heaped itself on me, my sufferings worse and unendingly worse, never managing to die, until all the warnings the monk had given in my dream were realized against me, as punishment for the weakness of my faith.

III

Despite this failing, by the mercy and favor of my masters I was allowed to ride home with them in the coach-and-six, drawn by the horses they'd just got in Voronezh, and once I'd gotten back into the swing of things I decided to get some crested doves – a cock and a hen to raise on a shelf in the stable. The cock was all clay-colored, but the hen – oh, that hen was such a beaut! With her white plumes and her red legs. I was crazy about them: sometimes the cock would coo in the night, what a lovely sound, and during the day they would flit around among the horses, pecking at seeds and trading kisses. Wonderful scenes, to a child.

And then one day amid all that kissing and cooing they decided to have chicks, and then those'd grow up and start cooing and kissing each other all over, and then more eggs'd hatch and more doves still. These baby dove chicks are so tiny, tiny and covered in yellow fluff, like mallow seed-pods you might find in the grass, or that children gather when they play "Cat Communion," except these have gigantic beaks, so big they look like Circassian princes! One day I began looking them over, my little doveys, and to make sure I didn't squish this one I picked him up by his little beak, and then I looked him over – looked and looked, once I started I couldn't stop looking at how soft and cute and sweet he was, but the cock was always trying to get him out of my hands. So I had a little fun with him, teasing the cock with his chick; but afterward when I went to put the little guy back in the nest, I saw he'd stopped breathing. Just my luck! I cupped my hands around him and tried to breathe on him for warmth, hoping to see him pull through – but no, dead is dead, and dead he was! Now I was all worked up – I scooped him up and flung him through the window. There was another one left in the nest. Then a white cat materialized out of nowhere, snatched up the dead one, and vanished. But not before I got a good look at her: white all over, but for a black patch on her head as though she was wearing a hat. I said to myself, to hell with the cat, let her eat the poor dead thing. But then that night I awoke with a terrible start from the sound of that dove getting into a terrible row on the shelf over my bed. I looked up, and what scene did the moon cast her light on but that same scrawny white cat, this time dragging off my other chick, the live one!

What's the big idea, I thought, who do you think you are! I threw my riding boot at her, but she jumped out of the way, carrying off my poor little chick. Probably to dinner! My doves were sad at first, and spent a while grieving after their babies, but soon they were kissing and cooing again and they had more chicks still, and wouldn't you know, that same damned cat showed up again! The devil knows how she knew they'd hatched – must've had the stables under constant surveillance. So one day I come in and there I see her in the middle of dragging another of the chicks off – this is in broad daylight – and she did it so stealthily I never had a chance to throw anything after her. I decided to teach her a lesson, so I set a trap on the windowsill; no sooner did that mangy head poke into the room than she was trapped for the night, gazing off and meowing pitifully. When I got there, I opened the trap and flung her face-first into my boot, so she wouldn't be able to get at me with those claws, and then I held her by her hind legs and her tail with my left hand while I took my whip from the wall with my right, and then sat down on the bed. Now I began to thrash the daylights out of her. I must've smashed her a hundred and fifty times, good strong strokes, too, until her resistance gave out completely. Then, when it was all done, I hoisted her out of my boot. Suddenly I thought, uh-oh, have I killed her? How was I supposed to figure it out? I laid her down across the entryway, took up my little axe, and hacked off her tail. She let out a little "meeeew" and turned around ten times or so, then she scampered off.

Alright, I said, I have a feeling you'll be leaving my doves alone from now on. And just to be totally sure, I took the severed tail and nailed it to the wall outside my window – a very smart move, I thought. But an hour hadn't gone by, or maybe two at the most, before who do I see charging into the stables but the Countess's personal maid, who had never shown her mug around the stables before, and she was brandishing an umbrella at me, shouting, "Aha! Aha! So you're the one! It's you!"

"What are you talking about? What's me?"

"You're the one who hacked up poor Zozinka!" she said. "Or isn't that Zozinka's tail hanging next to your window!"

"Imagine making such a fuss, just because I have a cat's tail hanging near my window."

"Where do you get the nerve!" she said.

"Where do *I* get the nerve? Where does *she* get the nerve, eating up my dove chicks!"

"So that's what this is about?! Your pigeons!?"

"Listen, that pussy's nothing fancy either."

You understand, I was old enough that I'd heard such language already.

"What's a cat like that go for, by the pound?"

And that damned dragonfly, she answered, "Who do you imagine you are speaking to!? Don't you realize that that was my cat? Who purred in the lap of her Ladyship the Countess?!" and she gave me a slap across the face. I've always been pretty quick with my hands too, so I reached behind her, grabbed the dirty broom from behind the doors, and just like that, *smash*, thwacked her across the waist with it.

My goodness, what a big deal that turned out to be! They sent me right away to have a little trial before the manager, a German, and his sentence was that I be whipped as cruelly as possible, and then be moved from the stables to the English garden, where my work would consist of smashing stones in the path with a mallet… well, oh boy, did they beat me – a beating that burned with cruelty, so bad that I couldn't even stand when they were through, and had to be carried to my father on a tattered old mat. Still, that was no big deal, and what I really detested was the other part of my sentence, standing around in the road smashing pebbles with a mallet… this bored me to the point where I would just stand there, thoughts tumbling around, wondering what to do for myself, until finally I decided to put an end to my life. I got a strong cane rope from one of the footmen, waited for evening, took a bath, and went out to a copse of aspens behind the threshing floor, bent down to say a prayer in the name of all Christians, made a noose and tied it to the bough, put my head through. All that remained was for me to jump off, any second now, any second… this I had it in me to do, but no sooner did I spring from the bough and start sailing toward the ground than I realized I was already lying on the ground, facing up, and there was a gypsy standing over me, his brilliant white teeth flashing against the dark of the night and his face's dark skin.

"Well, my friend," he says, "what exactly are you up to?"

"What business is it of yours?"

"Can your life really be so bad," he goes on, "that it's worse than dying?"

"So it would seem," I say. "No picnic."

"Better than hang by your own hand," he tells me, "why don't you come and live with us? It's a different kind of hanging altogether."

"What's your story, what kind of life are we talking about? Who are you people, thieves?"

"Thieves," he says, "oh yes. Thieves and cons, that's our bag."

"I see. And I bet it happens, doesn't it, that sometimes you even cut a man's throat, when you have to?"

"Oh, it happens," he answers. "We get into it sometimes."

I thought and thought about what to do. At home, today was just like yesterday and tomorrow would be another today, and there I'd be, kneeling down with my little mallet, knock, knock, knocking away at my pebbles, knees and hands grown hard from the work. And all the while everyone laughing at me, at how that damned German had sentenced me to smash a whole mountain into rubble all for the tail of a cat. They were merciless: "You call yourself a savior! Saved his Lordship's life, did you?!" I just couldn't take any more of that, and, realizing that my only options till now had been life or death, with a wave of my hand and the shedding of a tear, I decided to become a highwayman.

IV

That tricky gypsy wouldn't give me a second to get a hold of myself.

"If you want me to trust you not to run home," he says, "you'll sneak off to the stables now, and bring back a pair of horses – good ones, yes, *magnificent* ones, the kind of horses we can run far through the night and into morning."

I was torn. I mean, I'm no thief, but you know how it is: when the devil calls you follow; and since I'd learned all the ins and outs of the stables already, it was no problem to sneak around behind the stackyard and grab two horses – such horses, nothing could exhaust them! – while the gypsy reached into his pocket and pulled out some amulets made from wolves' teeth, which he put around the horses' necks, and we jumped on and rode them off. The horses could smell the wolves' teeth, and I can't even tell you how fast they ran. By morning we were just a hundred versts from the town of Karachev. There, we had no trouble selling the horses off to the first yardman we could find, and we headed off the river to divvy up the money. We'd got three hundred rubles for the horses, all of it, as people got it in those days, in bank notes. The gypsy hands me a single silver ruble and he says, "Here, here's your cut."

This really got my goat: "I risk my neck stealing two horses, while you sit and watch without taking any risks – why should my share be so puny?"

"Because," he says, "that's just how big it got."

"Don't be an idiot," I say. "Why should you walk off with so much more?"

"I'll tell you again," he says, "it's because I'm the master, and you're the pupil."

"What do you mean, pupil?" I say. "A pupil! And you think it's all for you." One word follows another like this, and we argue for a long time. Finally I say, "I'm not riding any further with you, you're a scoundrel!"

"All right, buddy, you stay behind, just stay. Probably get me in trouble anyway: haven't even got papers."

And so we part company, and I set about going straight to the authorities and turn myself in for a runaway. But I only get as far as the clerk, and when I tell my story he says, "Oh, you fool, you fool! What do you want to turn yourself in for? Haven't you got ten rubles?"

"Well," I say, "I've got one silver ruble, but not ten."

"Okay, well maybe, maybe there's… something else. Let's see. Have you got a silver cross around your neck? Or – there, in your ear, is that an earring?"

"Yeah, a little one."

"Silver?"

"It's silver, plus I have a cross – I got it in Mitrofani, it's silver too."

"Well, get a move on, give them here," he says, "and I can write you up a discharge so you can move along to Nikolaev – they need a lot of people there, and tramps from these parts always seem to end up thereabouts."

So I gave him the ruble, the cross, and the earring; he wrote a Certificate of Discharge and made it official with a stamp. Then he says, "You know, there ought to be an extra charge for the stamp – everyone pays that, but I feel sorry for how poor you are, and I don't want my handiwork confiscated for lack of the appropriate notarization, so just take it and get out of here. And if you run into anyone else I can help out – send them my way."

"Oh, yeah," I think to myself, "a real guardian angel, that one. Feels sorry for me! So sorry he takes the cross right off my neck!" I didn't send him anyone, just kept moving on in the name of Christ, not a red cent to my name.

When I got to the city, I headed straight for the marketplace to look for work. Very few guys had come down that day – all told, there were three of them, besides me, and they must all have been vagabonds too. But there was a big crowd looking for workers, and twisting and yanking us toward them, one after the other. One gentleman pounced right on me, a guy so big you wouldn't believe it, bigger than me even, just knocked his way through to me, grabbed me by both arms, and dragged me off behind him, knocking the crowd out of the way with his fist, and cursing like a sailor, though I could see that his eyes were welling with tears. He took me to his house, heaped together from whatever had been lying around, and then he says, "Be honest with me – you a runaway?"

I say, "A runaway, yes."

"Well," he says, "what are you – a thief? A murderer? Or just some drifter?"

"What's with the interrogation?"

"Oh, I'm just trying to figure out what kind of work you'll be suited for."

So I told him my whole sad story, about the life of hardship I'd escaped from, and he ran right over to kiss me and said, "I have just the thing for a man like you, just the thing! Since you're so caring with those birds of yours, I'll retain you to be a nanny to my little girl!"

I was horrified. "What are you talking about – a nanny?! Let me assure you – I'm not cut out for it!"

"Oh, nonsense, nonsense. I can tell just by looking at you that you'd make a good nanny. And I'm in a terrible bind: you see, my wife left me, just galloped off one day with a cavalry officer, and left her little daughter here for me to look after. I have no time to feed her and no food besides, but now you can take responsibility for her and I'll pay you a retainer of two rubles per month."

"I beg your pardon," I answer, "but the two rubles have nothing to do with it – how could I possibly bear up under such a responsibility?"

"Oh, nonsense," he says. "You're a real Russian, aren't you? Well, a Russian can bear up under anything!"

"Yes, you have a good point, of course I'm a real

Russian. But I'm a man, as you can see, so I'm… not much for breastfeeding."

"Oh, it's no problem," he says, "I can help you out with that. I'll find some old Jew to buy a goat off of: all you have to do is milk it and feed that to my daughter." I thought it through a minute.

"Sir, one can of course nurse a child with the help of a goat; all the same, I think the help of a woman is better."

"No," he says, "and don't ever talk to me about women: they're the bringers of all the strife and ruin in the world! Besides, if you won't agree to raise my daughter I'll call the Cossacks right away, how do you like that? I'll have them bind you up and cart you to the police house to be sent back where you came from. So choose now, which do you prefer: go back home to your little Count to smash rocks in the garden path all day, or raise my daughter for me?"

I thought about it a minute. No, no, it was too late to go back. I agreed to become a nanny. That very day we found some Jew and bought a nannygoat off him, and her kid. I slaughtered the kid, and my new employer and I ate him with some noodles, and I milked the nannygoat and started feeding it to the baby. The baby was tiny and foul and pitiful, always squealing. My boss, her father, was a petty bureaucrat who came from Poles. Never home, the little scallawag, always running to friends' houses to play cards, leaving me alone with my charge, that little girl, and I started getting real used to having her around – the boredom was unbearable, so we began to play together, and finally I was spending most of my time on her. I'd lay her down in the little wooden tub and give her a nice little bath, and if she got a rash someplace I'd gently sprinkle some flour over it, and I'd comb her tender little head, or rock her to sleep on my lap, and, when cabin fever got really bad, I'd throw on a big coat and put her inside it and walk to the bay to wash her diapers. The goat even got so used to being around us that she'd walk with us too. That's how I lived until summer fell again, my little child growing, even started standing on her own wobbly legs, but I noticed that she was bow-legged. I wanted to show this to my boss, but he didn't care at all: "Well, what am I supposed to do about it? If you're so concerned, go find a healer, let him take a look."

So that's exactly what I did. And the healer said, "She has the English Sickness. You need to cover her with sand."

And that's what I started doing. I found a pretty little spot on the shore of the bay with lots of sand, and on serene, balmy days we'd all go over there, the goat, the baby, and me. I'd rake the warm sand and bury her up to her waist in it, and then give her some sticks and pebbles to play with, and our goat would wander circles around us munching on the grass, and me? I'd sit and sit with my hands in my lap until my lids began getting heavy, and then I'd take a little nap.

The three of us spent whole days this way, and not a few of them, and they were the best antidote I found to the horrible loneliness I felt, which as I've said oppressed me terribly, and after a while, especially when spring began and I would bury her and nap by the bay, I started having the most cockamamie dreams. Just as soon as I'd drift off, the bay roaring beside me, a warm wind rolling down from the steppe and coming over me, I would feel a strange mystical awareness and be given over to all sorts of terrible visions: strange steppes of some kind, with horses, and some voice always calling me over: "Ivan! Ivan! Come here, Ivan, brother!" I'd give a start, wake up flinching, and spit: "Hey, *ptooey*, there's no deep meaning buried here! What are you calling me for?" I'd look around: heavy, slow melancholy, the goat already far off, wandering, nibbling grass, and the baby buried in sand, and nothing else… oh, how dreadfully boring! A desert there, the sun on the bay, and no sooner would I drift off again than the breeze would welter in with its strange enchantment, a voice climbing higher and higher in my soul, "Ivan! Come, brother Ivan!" I'd even swear, I'd say back, "Well, show yourself already! Who the devil are you, and what do you want from me?" There was one time I got really angry like that, sitting there half-asleep looking over the bay, when suddenly an airy little cloud comes up over the horizon and starts flying directly toward me. I shout, "Hey, you there, where do you think you're going? You planning on soaking me?" And then all of a sudden what do I see standing before me but that monk, from long ago, the one with the old-lady face, the one I had killed with my whip!

I say, "Go away! Get back to Hell with you!" And he just keeps tenderly calling out: "Come on, Ivan, my brother, come on! There's so much you'll have to endure before you can attain it!" In the dream I curse him and say, "Where are you trying to take me, and what more will I have to endure?" And he suddenly turns back into a cloud and lights himself from within to show me a vision of I don't even know what: a steppe, strange people, true savages, Saracens, the kinds of things one finds in the tales of Yeruslan, or the Crown Prince Bova, in big shaggy hats, armed with arrows, riding terrible, savage horses. And while I saw this there was also a sound of guffawing, and neighing, and wild laughter... sand billowed up into a cloud that grew to engulf everything, somewhere in the distance a bell tolling faintly, and the light of a crimson dawn poured over a giant white monastery that appeared, its walls patrolled by angels with wings and golden spears, and whenever one of them banged his spear into his shield, the sea around the monastery would start to roil and seethe, and from its depths a chorus of ghostly voices would cry up: "Holy!"

I think to myself, *seems this whole monk business is starting up again!* And the annoyance of it woke me, only to see an old woman, of the gentlest countenance, kneeling over my little mistress, wringing her hands and weeping to put the sea out of business.

I stared a long time at her, thinking to myself, *I suppose I must still be in the vision, eh?* but as some time passed and I saw she didn't disappear, I got to my feet and stumbled a bit toward her – well, would you believe that the next thing I knew the old lady had dug that girl out of the sand and was cradling her in her arms, kissing her and crying and crying and kissing?

So I ask, "Can I help you?"

But she charges at me, the baby clasped tight against her breast, all the while hissing, "This is my child, my daughter, my daughter!"

I say, "Well, what do you expect me to do about it?"

"I expect you," she replied, "to give her over to me."

"You must tell me where you got the idea I'd be doing that!"

"Really now! Have you no pity? You can see for yourself, how she clings to me."

"Clings to you? Oh boy. Listen, she's just a dumb little kid – she clings like that to me too! At any rate, you're not walking off with her."

"And why not?"

"Because, can't you see, she's been entrusted to me! Look, there's the little goat who comes on our walks with us. Now I must return the girl to her father."

This old woman began to cry and to clasp at her hands:

"Alright," she says, "listen, if you won't give the child back to me, at least don't go telling my husband – that great Master of yours – that you've seen me, but come back to this same spot again tomorrow, with the girl, so I can cradle her some more."

"Now that's a bird of another stripe. This I can, and promise you I will, do."

And sure enough, I made it home without saying so much as a word to the boss, and, come next morning, I took the goat and the little girl back to the bay, where the old lady was already waiting. She was sitting in a little dimple of earth, and no sooner had she caught sight of us than she bounded over, crying and laughing and shoving toys into the kid's hands, even hanging a tinkly little bell on a red ribbon around our little goat's neck, and she handed me a pipe and a pouch of tobacco and a comb.

"Please," she says, "have a few puffs on this pipe, and I'll look after the baby."

And this is how it was for all the meetings we started having: the lady would occupy herself with the child, and I would laze off into a sleep, or sometimes she would start making an account of herself... how she had been offered to my master in marriage against her will... by would you believe it her evil stepmother... how she had never liked this husband of hers... how she could never manage to love him. But then one man, this other one, the cavalry officer, whoever he was – *him* she loved, and she could only complain of how she'd been given against her will to this other man. "And my husband," she explained, "you know, he leads a very indecent life, all kinds of dealings with this one and that one... And this other man? His fine whiskers, his clothes always clean – I could really have been happy with him," she'd say, "except, no I couldn't really, because I'd just miss my baby. And now me and him have come back to town, and we're staying in the apartment of a friend of his, but I live in terror that my husband will find out and we'll have to leave town, and then I'll be torn from my baby girl once again!"

"My dear, what did you expect? If you, having disdained the laws of God and man alike, insist on carrying on in this backward way, you should expect to suffer!"

But then she started to cry, and one time, one day, she started blubbering even more pitiably than usual, and all the wailing was really starting to get intolerable, when just out of the clear blue sky she started promising me lots of money. Sure enough, it came time for our final meeting and she said to me, "Listen, Ivan," as you see she already knew my name, "listen to what I'm going to tell you: he's coming here himself, on his way to us right now."

"Who is? What do you mean?"

"My cavalry officer."

"Terrific. What's it to me?"

She promptly started spinning some yarn about how he'd just won a bunch of money at cards, and how he cared so much for her happiness that he wanted to pay me a thousand rubles just to return her daughter to her.

"But that," I say, "is never going to happen."

"Well why not, Ivan? Why in heaven not? Don't you have any pity for us, seeing how we're torn in two like this!"

"Lady, pity or no pity, I can't be bought for a big price any easier than a little one. It's just as well your cavalry officer keeps his rubles and I will keep your daughter."

She cries more, so I say, "You might as well stop bawling, since I don't give a damn."

"You're heartless, you! You're made of stone!"

"I'm not stone in the least," I answer, "I'm flesh and bone, like you or anyone else. But also a man of good faith and responsibility: it's my job to keep this child, and keep her I shall."

She was really pulling out all the stops, trying to

convince me: "Can't you see that the child will be happier with me?"

"Once again," I answered, "that's none of my business."

"Are you saying," she started squealing, "are you saying that I have to be separated again from my little girl?!"

"If you, having disdained the laws of God and man…"

But I didn't have a chance to finish what I wanted to say, because just then a light little Uhlan came walking towards us up the steppe. Back in those days army officers had real panache, and they'd walk with true military dignity, not like the ones we have now, who go around disguised as clerks. So this Uhlan cavalry officer is trundling on over, hands at his sides, greatcoat slung widely across his shoulders… no strength in him at all, maybe, but a fierce fancy haircut… I look this newcomer over and I think, "It'd sure be nice to play around with this guy, pass a little time, at least." And I decided that if he said so much as a word to me, I'd insult him the worst way I possibly could, so that hopefully, God willing, we could get into some really good goddamn fisticuffs. I had to take a minute just to appreciate how great that sounded, and I tuned out that whimpering old bag completely; now I really just wanted to have a little fun.

V

No sooner had I decided to amuse myself a little than I thought: "How best to get a rise out of him, so he hits me first?" I took a seat and pulled the comb out of my pocket, and I made like I was going to comb my hair. The officer, meantime, walks straight over to his lady.

She's just *blah blah blah, blah blah*, on and on about how I'm keeping her baby from her.

He just strokes her head and says, "Don't you worry about that, my dear, not at all: I have ways of making him agree. We'll just wave the money in front of him," he says, "and if that doesn't do the trick? We simply take the child." And just as he says this he walks over and hands me a huge wad of banknotes and says, "there's exactly a thousand rubles rolled up there. Now just hand over the child, and you can keep it and go wherever you want."

But as I was being deliberately rude to him, I didn't answer right away – first I got up real slow, then I clipped the comb onto my belt, and only then did I clear my throat and say: "No. No," I say, "maybe this would buy you. Maybe for you people this represents honor," and I grabbed the bills right out of his hand, spat on them, and threw them to the ground. "Now be a good boy and clean up this mess."

He flushed red with rage, and came at me – but, as you can see for yourselves, no army officer could hold out long against a man built like I am: I barely had to so much as tap him and he went flying, his spurs soaring up over his head, saber spinning out beneath him. Now I stomped my foot down on his saber and said: "That's what you get – all your courage pressed under my heel!"

He may have been a weakling, but the little officer had stones – as soon as he realized he wasn't going to get his little dagger back from me, he unclasped himself from it and came at me with flying little fists, the old hound. Of course, he got nothing but punishment. Still, I admired him – a proud and noble man. I wouldn't accept his money, and he didn't stop to pick it up, either.

When we'd stopped fighting, I shouted at him, "Oh, why don't you just take the money already Your Grace! It'll come in handy from time to time."

What do you think happened next? – He left the money lying there and ran right for the child and grabbed one of her legs! So I of course grab the other and I said, "Go ahead, give a pull – we'll see who ends up with the bigger half!"

He shouted, "You scoundrel, you scoundrel, you villain!" and spat right into my face. Left the child, set himself about comforting the lady, who was wailing with the most desperately pitiful cries, and reaching back against the force he dragged her with, casting her miserable eyes and desperate hands at me and the child. I could see how she was torn in two – one half going with him, the other with the child. Just at that minute, suddenly who did I see making his way from town but the old man who'd hired me, running over with a pistol in his hands, which he promptly started firing while he yelled out, "Stop them, Ivan! Stop them!"

"Why should I?" I think to myself. "Really, what's to gain by stopping them? Let them be free to love each other!" And so I caught up with the lady and her Uhlan, gave them the girl, and said, "Here, take the little urchin! Only now you'll have to take me, also," I explained, "because my papers are faked."

And she says, "Yes, dear Ivan, let's go, let's go together! You can come live with us."

So we galloped off, carrying the little girl with us, and leaving for my master the goat and the money.

The whole way to Penza, as I sat riding on the box of these gentry folk's coach, I kept thinking, had I done the right thing, beating that officer like that? After all, he had taken a sacred oath, and in wartime had probably defended the fatherland with that very saber, and the very Emperor himself, according to the table of ranks, was required to address him in the formal. And I, idiot, I had thrashed him senseless! After a while, another thought boiled up: where was fate going to lead me now? A fair was coming through Penza just then, and the Uhlan said to me:

"Listen, Ivan, I hate to say it, but I can't afford to keep you on."

I say, "Why not!"

And he answers, "Because I'm a government official, and you have no passport of any kind."

"That's not exactly true," I say. "I had a passport, it's just that it was fake."

"At any rate, you haven't even got that one now. So here, take this – two hundred rubles for you – and hit the road, just go with God anywhere He takes you."

This came as a real shock, mind you, and my heart got pretty heavy because I'd grown pretty soft on that little girl. I didn't want to go anywhere. But I could see this was the only way, so I said, "Then accept my humble thanks for the cash. There's just one more thing."

"What?"

"It's just – I'm sorry I was so rude to you, and that I beat on you like that."

He let out a chuckle. "It's alright, God bless you. You're a pretty good guy."

"No, no," I answered. "It has nothing to do with how good a guy I am. I can't go around with this weighing on my conscience! You're a defender of the fatherland, who, for all I know, the Emperor himself addresses in the formal."

"Well, that's true," he answered. "When we get our commissions, they write in one part: *On our authority you are to be treated by all persons with honor and respect.*"

"So as you can imagine then," I say, "nothing can stop my gnawing guilt now."

"Well, what of it? You're stronger and you beat me; it's not like you can take back the punches you landed."

"It's true," I said, "I can't. But at least it'd ease my conscience if you'd oblige me by taking a couple of swings at me." I puffed out my cheeks and stood in front of him.

"But what for?" he says. "Why in the world should I start hitting you?"

"Just to ease my conscience, so that my humiliating the officer of my Emperor won't go unpunished!"

He burst out laughing, but I got back in front of him and puffed my cheeks out again, as fat as I could.

He asked me, "What are you puffing your cheeks like that for, and what's with the faces?"

I answered, "This is how the soldiers do it, all according to strictures of procedure. Please, come at me from both sides!" and I puffed my cheeks back out. Only suddenly, when he was supposed to be smashing me, he jumped up instead to give me a kiss. "Oh, for Christ's sake, that's enough, Ivan, enough: there's no reason on God's earth why I should hit you even once – just get yourself out of here, before Mashinka and the girl get back and start crying all over you."

"Ah! Well that, sir, is another matter – why upset them?" And so, much as I wanted to stay, I headed out as fast as I could, without even excusing myself, got out the gate, and stopped, and thought to myself, "Where to now?"

To be honest, I couldn't help thinking about how, for all the time that had passed since I'd run off from my masters, I still had no place to settle down and warm my hands. "The jig is up," I thought. "I'll go down to the police headquarters and turn myself in. Except," I thought, "what a perfect waste, now that I finally have a little money, to let the police take all of it. Let me have a little pleasure from it first; let me find a tavern and have a little tea with biscuits. Then I'll turn myself in." So I found the tavern on the fairgrounds, ordered some tea and biscuits, and sat there a long time drinking, until there was nothing I could do to drag it out any longer. I stepped out for a stroll and walked across the River Sura into the steppe, where the horse fair was set up among the crooked little tents of Tatars. All of these looked identical, except one that was gaily festooned with all different colors, and around it a lot of different gentlemen were busying themselves trying out saddle horses. There were all sorts – military, civilians, and landowners who'd come to the fair specially, all standing around, smoking pipes, and in the middle of them on a rug of splendid colors sat a tall Tatar of the steppe, skinny as a blade of grass, wearing a great robe and a golden skullcap. I just sort of stared off for a minute, till I saw someone I'd been drinking tea with back at the tavern and asked him what the deal was with this big-shot Tatar, why he was sitting all off to himself in the middle. And the guy responded:

"What's the matter, don't you know him? That's Djangar Khan!"

"Who exactly is Djangar Khan, then?!"

He answered, "Djangar Khan is the steppe's greatest horse breeder. His herds run all the way from the Volga to the Urals, across the sands of the Ryn, and Djangar Khan rules over the steppe just like a Tsar!"

"Hold on," I say. "Isn't the steppe ours?"

"In a manner of speaking," he answers. "It's ours alright, except we can't do a damn thing with it, since it's nothing but salt flats sweeping out toward the Caspian, that or endless grasses or birds taking wing under the heavens, and our officials can't do a damned thing out there," he says, "and so Djangar Khan rules the land, and they say that he has his sheikhs and vice-sheikhs out there, all across Asia, and dervishes and Uhlans, and he gives orders to them as he sees fit, and they're always glad to oblige."

As I heard these words, I saw that a little Tatar boy had at the same time brought a small white mare before the Khan and started muttering something; and the Khan got to his feet, grabbed a long-handled whip, and stood right in front of the horse's head, the whip leaning into her forehead. How can I describe the way that barbarian looked? Just like a magnificent statue, the kind that commands all your attention, and you could see from the look of him that he was seeing straight into that horse's wild heart. And since I myself had been judging horses since childhood, I could read the situation and see that the horse too recognized in him an expert, and was standing up as if to say, "Well, well, get a look at what a magnificent animal I am!" This was how he, this Tatar of the steppe, looked the horse over – not walking around her, as our officers are prone to do, unable to stand still for any time at all, but just staring from one place until suddenly he dropped the whip, wordlessly kissed his fingers one after the other. A real beaut! And again he walked over to the carpet, crossing his legs as he sat, and the mare pricked up her ears, snorted, and began playing.

The gentlemen standing around now started trying to bargain: one offered a hundred rubles, another a hundred and fifty, and so on, all of them struggling to outbid each other. The horse was, in fact, magnificent, not so big, like an Arabian, but well built, with a little head, eyes full as apples, and sharp little ears; her flanks resonant, even airy, her back straight as an arrow, and legs just as light and swift as you can imagine. I couldn't tear my eyes from her. Djangar Khan, seeing what an enchantress he had on his hands, and how everyone was struggling to bid more and more on her, nodded at the grubby little Tatar boy, who hopped right on and started putting her through her paces – sitting in that distinctive Tatar way, pressing into her with his knees, and she just flew off like a bird, not a flash of unsteadiness. Periodically he'd lean up over her little head and holler, and when he did she would just burn off into the distance, disappearing into a cloud of sand. "Oh, you serpent!" I thought to myself, "little steppe bustard! Oh, you lovely thing, where could such a horse possibly have been sired?" I could feel my heart welling up with desire for her, for that impeccable horse, all my native passions inflamed. Then the Tatar boy returned her, and she gave a little snort through both nostrils, until she was all out of air, and she was completely tired out and wouldn't give another sound. "Oh, my little dear," I thought, "my pretty one!" It seemed to me that I'd have surrendered my soul and sold my own father and mother to have her, but how could I possibly afford such a little jet, with all those noblemen and army procurers falling all over each other and ratcheting up God knows how high a price for her? But even this was nothing, when suddenly, before the courser was even sold, a rider approached gallantly on a black steed, in from Selixa on the other side of the Sura, waving a wide-brimmed hat. And then he jumped off his horse and made straight for the white mare, stood before her like another statue, and said, "The mare is mine."

The Great Khan answered, "You're very wrong, my friend. These gentlemen here are offering me five hundred for her."

But the horseman, a massive, paunchy Tatar, his face burnt by the sun and peeling, his eyes like little crumbs, hollered, "I'm offering a hundred more than anyone else!"

The gentlemen refused to be bested and just kept upping their bids, while that dry Djangar Khan just sat there pursing his lips. Another Tatar appeared, charging from the other side of the Sura on a chestnut horse, and he was another one marked by the desert, skinny, jaundiced, and seemingly keener than the first on getting that horse. He glided off his mount and planted himself unmoving before the white mare and said, "I'm letting all of you know it: I've set my mind on making the mare mine!"

I asked the guy next to me how it was all going to wind up. He said, "It's all in the giant hands of the great Djangar Khan. He's an old hand at trickery like this. Every fair he comes to, he begins by offering up the more ordinary horses, at pretty reasonable prices. Then, his last day in camp, he produces one or two of these magnificent beasts, as though by magic, so magnificent that the connoisseurs just go crazy. And he, that canny Tatar, presides over the whole affair and stretches it all as far as it can go, and finally pulls in a terrific price. Everyone's already keen to this trick, and they wait around for those last horses – here you see what happens when he finally produces them. Everyone thinks the Khan is leaving today – and he will, when night falls – but meanwhile, just look at what a mare he's brought out…"

"You're telling me," I shouted. "What a horse!"

"She's a beauty, alright. I've heard that he drove her here in the middle of a huge herd, so that the only ones who saw her were the other horses, and nobody knew a thing about her except these two Tatars that just arrived, and even them he deceived by saying that this one's not for sale, and at night he had her separated from the others and sent off to graze in a special wood in Mordovia with his most expert herdsmen, and now just like that he summons her and announces she's for sale. Just you wait and see what a hullaballoo this horse raises, and what a price he'll get, the old dog. In fact, would you like to bet on it, on who'll ride her off, I mean?"

"What do you mean, friend? Why should we bet on such a thing?"

"Because it's fun, and because we already know something about the outcome – for, mark my words, soon all these fine gentlemen will be bowing out, and the mare will go to one of those two Asiatics over there."

"What's their story?" I ask. "Are they so rich?"

"Very rich indeed," he responded, "and accomplished huntsmen both. They drive their herds to every fair, and if they see any horses they like, they'll flog each other mercilessly to get them. Everybody around here knows them: the pot-bellied one with the peeling face, that one's called Bakshey Otuchev, and that other one, the skinny bag of bones over there, is Chepkun Yemgurcheyev – both of them are wicked on the hunt, now just you watch what they'll do for a little fun."

I quieted down for a second and looked: sure enough, the gentlemen who'd been haggling and bidding for the horse had backed away, while those two Tatars were jockeying to get near Djangar Khan, pushing each other out of the way and grabbing at his hands, and neither would let go of the mare for a second, shaking and screaming, and one of them shouted:

"Besides the money, I'll throw in five head!" by which he meant five horses, and the other one yelled: "The devil take your lying muzzle into the ground, I'll offer ten!"

Bakshey Otushev shouted, "Fine, then – fifteen!"

And Chepkun Yemgurcheyev: "Twenty!"

Bakshey: "Twenty-five!"

And Chepkun: "Thirty!"

But it seemed neither of them had the horses to offer more than that. Chepkun had offered thirty, and Bakshey now offered thirty too, but no more; but since next Chepkun threw in a saddle, Bakshey offered a saddle and a riding gown. Then Chepkun added a gown to his offer, and they grew silent for a minute, trying to figure out how to top one another. Chepkun shouted, "Listen, Djangar Khan, I'm going home, and as soon as I get there I'll send you one of my daughters," so that Bakshey also offered his daughter, and they were at loggerheads once again. Suddenly the others broke the silence they'd been watching in, and it seemed all Tatardom was whooping and hollering in its own barbarous tongue. They tried to pull the two bidders apart, to save them from destroying each other, and then stood there, pulling them, this Chepkun and Bakshey, as far apart as they could, and gave them a good talking-to, poking them in the ribs and trying to get them to consider a different approach.

I asked the guy next to me, "Please tell me, what's going on over there?"

"Well," he replied, "those fellows pulling them apart are noble princes, and they feel sorry for Chepkun and Bakshey, they want to find any way they can of persuading either one to let the other have the horse."

"How can anyone possibly expect them to give up struggling over this horse they both obviously like so much? It'll never happen!"

"Oh, you've got them pegged wrong," my neighbor answered. "These Asiatics, they're a reasonable, powerful people. They'll decide instead of wrecking each other to give Djangar Khan whatever he asks, and then by common consent they'll declare the horse a prize in their little contest."

Now that got my attention: "Tell me, friend, what do you mean *contest*?"

"No need to ask, just keep watching – it's hard to explain it, and besides, they're about to begin!"

I looked and saw that Chepkun and Bakshey both seemed to have simmered down, and had been released from the grips of those Tatar peacemakers who had separated them. They both charged, ran up to each other and touched fists.

"It's a deal!" one of them said, and then the other one likewise answered, "Yup, it's a deal."

Both of them promptly cast off their coats and tunics and leather slippers, and then their cotton shirts, and dropped to the dirt, sitting across from each other, two sandpipers of the steppe, and just waited.

I'd never before seen anything like this, and I was rapt. What incredible tricks were these heathens up to? They grasped each other firmly, left hand in left hand, legs extended in front of them, resting their feet against each other, and shouted: "Let's go!"

I couldn't even guess where they planned on going, but a handful of Tatar voices called back:

"We're ready, guys, we're ready."

And then a hobbled old Tatar man emerged from the crowd, a distinguished-looking sort with two serious whips in his hands. He held them up to each other and showed Chepkun, Bakshey, and the whole crowd: "As you can see, they are of the same length."

"Yes, yes, they're the same!" the Tatars clamored. "We can all see that they're well-crafted, the same length, sure. Now let them sit down and begin!"

Bakshey and Chepkun were already wriggling in anticipation of getting their hands on the whips.

That same impressive old Tatar said to them, "Wait!' He handed one whip to each man, then clapped his hands quietly three times: one, two three... and no sooner did he reach the third clap than Bakshey lashed out at Chepkun with a severe thwack across his back and shoulder, and Chepkun came back with a similar crack. So they went abusing each other that way: staring into each other's eyes, soles of their feet pressed against each other, left hand in left hand, while with their right hands flogging each other mercilessly. And, sweet heaven, what a serious whipping they dealt each other! One would get a really strong hit, and then the other would reply with an even harsher one. They just went on like that, until their eyes were screaming with intensity and their left hands froze up, and still neither of them would surrender.

I asked my friend, "So this is what they do, just go at it till someone wins, like two gentlemen at a duel?"

"Yes," he answered. "It's just like hand-to-hand combat for them, except they're fighting not for their honor but to stave off a financial loss."

"And how long can they just sit there clobbering each other?"

"For as long as they choose, or until their strength gives out."

Meantime they just went on thrashing each other, and little arguments began breaking out among the crowd, some people saying "Chepkun will destroy Bakshey," while others argued, "Bakshey will flog Chepkun to oblivion," and the ones who were so disposed started placing little bets, some for Chepkun, some for Bakshey, depending on whose chances they liked better. They'd look to the fire in each man's eyes, at the flash of his teeth, his spine, all to gather subtle signals at who the odds favored. The man I'd been speaking to seemed to have witnessed a great many fights like this one, and though he had started out backing Bakshey, he now exclaimed, "Ah, there it goes, my twenty kopecks: Chepkun's going to thrash Bakshey."

"How can you even tell? It's impossible to decide – they're running totally even!"

"It's true," he replied, "that they're still both sitting upright and they seem well-matched. But they have different strategies."

"Alright then – but it seems to me that Bakshey's lashings are fiercer."

"That's true," he said, "but good news it isn't. No, I can kiss those kopecks good-bye: Chepkun's going to break him."

Well, this, I thought, *is such a weird situation. This new friend of mine's all confused. And yet he must be an old hand at this, making a bet like that!* So by now I had become intensely curious, you know, and probably something of a nuisance to my friend.

"Tell me, my dear man, what makes you so apprehensive about Bakshey's chances?"

"Oh, you weak little bumpkin! Take a look at Bakshey's back."

So I did: nothing seemed out of the ordinary. His back was virile and strong, as big and plump as a pillow.

"Can't you see how he strikes?"

I looked, and saw that he was hitting viciously, his eyes bulging out of his head, the whip drawing blood each time it landed.

"Just try and imagine what he's got going on in his guts."

"What do you mean 'his guts'? All I can see is that he's sitting up straight, his whole mouth wide open, taking in air in quick little gasps."

"That's what his problem is: his back is broad, and every stroke lands across it; he's laboring a whole hell of a lot, and that's making him pant; he's breathing through a big wide-open mouth, and that means all his insides will get struck by the air."

"Does that mean Chepkun's in the lead?"

"Oh, it's quite clear that he is – take a look. He's bone-dry, with not an ounce of fat on him, so his back is all scooped-out like the hold of a ship, which means no blow can land across the entire thing, but will only hit a couple spots. Meanwhile, you can see that he's striking Bakshey at a pretty good pace, not in a hurry, taking a breath between lashes, so that the whip doesn't land with too heavy a bonk, just enough to raise a welt. That's why that one's back, Bakshey's I mean, is all swelled up and turned dark purple like someone's teapot, but without a drop of blood on it – which means all the pain's lingering inside him. Now look at Chepkun – his back's cracking like he was a pig on a spit, so all the pain can be collected in his blood and ooze out while he destroys Bakshey. Make sense now?"

"Aha," I said. "Yes, now I get it." I immediately understood much about this strange sport and became really interested in it, especially in what the best way to act in a tricky situation might be.

"But really the most important thing," my friend went on, "is to see how that damned Chepkun keeps pace with that godawful ugly mug of his. Look – first he strikes, then he takes the next strike in retaliation, and blinks his eyes while it lands – that's a lot better than staring intensely like Bakshey. And see? Chepkun's clenched his teeth, too, and bitten his lip – that's a lot better, because by keeping his mouth sealed he stops anything from getting in and burning his insides."

I took careful note of this, and as I began to stare more intensely at Chepkun and Bakshey I came to understand all the more clearly that Bakshey was bound to lose, because his eyes had gone vacant and his lips had curled into a tight, open grin… I was exactly right: Bakshey hit Chepkun about twenty more times, each blow weaker than the last, until – *slam*! – he got all wobbly for a second, and then let Chepkun go, while his right hand still rose and fell as though he were whipping someone with it, but senselessly, gathering himself into a swoon. Well, at this my new friend proclaimed: "That's that! I'm down twenty kopecks!" And all the Tatars starting jabbering, congratulating Chepkun, and shouting: "Ay, good work Chepkun Yemgurcheyev, oh, you clever old rascal! Knocked poor Bakshey right out of his wits. Well, let's go, hop on – she's your mare now!"

Even Djangar Khan himself stood up from his rug, sucked on his lips for a minute, and said, "All yours, Chepkun, she's all yours! Climb on, you can catch your breath on her back!"

Chepkun got up: blood was oozing all down his back, but, I'll tell you, if he was in pain you'd never know it. He laid his robe and tunic over the horse's back, hoisted himself up, and rode off just like that. Again, I became lonely and bored.

"That's that," I thought. "I should probably get back to figuring out what to make of myself" – and the mere thought set me ashiver with worry.

But then, thank goodness, my new friend said to me, "Wait, wait, don't shove off just yet – something else is sure to happen here."

"What more could happen?" I asked. "It's all over."

"No," he said, "it's not over, just you take a look over there. See how Djangar Khan is puffing away on that pipe of his? Have no doubt, he's cooking up *something* – those Asiatics are always pulling tricks."

I thought to myself, "Ah, if only something like this would happen again! If I could find someone to pay for the horse, I'd never disappoint him!"

VI

What do you know! Everything happened just how I wanted: while Djangar Khan stood around blazing on that pipe of his, a Tatar boy appeared out of a clearing in the wood, galloping up not on a mare like the one Chepkun had taken from Bakshey for all the world to see, but on a bay colt, such a horse that it can't be described. If you've ever watched a corn crake tracing the boundary between fields – a corn crake or, as we called them back in Orlovsky, a landrail – well, if you've watched one fly, you'll know they have a way of spreading out their wings while their tails hang down, along with their legs, like they had no use for any of them, so they look like they're riding across the sky in an invisible carriage. This horse was like one of those birds, steaming forward on a power not totally his own.

I'm not telling tales when I say he wasn't just flying along, but even the earth itself was only creeping up behind him. Never had I seen a horse fly like this, and I couldn't even imagine the cost of such a prize, what treasure I could trade for him or who could be worthy of owning such a horse, what Prince had a stable worthy of him, and it never even occurred to me to dream that someday he might become mine.

"How did he become yours?" the spellbound listeners interrupted their narrator.

"How indeed, gentlemen! Mine, he became all mine, but just for a single moment, and if you'll be so kind as to continue indulging me, I'll tell the whole story."

The gentlemen as usual began to haggle over the horse, including my cavalry officer, to whom I'd given the little girl; but bargaining against all of them with equal impunity was a Tatar called Savakirey, short, stocky, but strong, wild, his head shaved until it looked like it'd been turned on a lathe, round and ruddy as a little head of cabbage, kisser like a red carrot, all in all you could say he looked fresh from the garden. He shouts, "Why empty your pockets for nothing? Let anyone who wants to cough up whatever the Khan's asking, and then let him face off against me at flogging! We'll see who wins the horse."

Naturally, none of the gentlemen took up his challenge – after all, what should they do, go up against a mad Tatar, sure to flog each and every one of them straight into the hereafter? My cavalry officer wasn't exacting rolling in it, just then, having lost a lot at the card table in Penza, but I could see how much he wanted the horse. I tugged at his sleeve and pulled him over to say, "Listen, no need to go round and round with these guys, just offer up whatever the Khan wants, and I'll sit down with this Savakirey and throttle him here in front of everyone!" He balked, but I insisted, told him, "Do it as a favor. I want to fight this guy."

So he did.

"So you and this Tatar... well, did you – what? Flog each other?"

"Oh, for sure! I gave him such a smashing, there in front of everybody – and the colt was mine to take."

"So you beat the Tatar?"

"Oh, I beat him alright. Not without a fight, mind you. But I overpowered him."

"Why, the pain must have been unbearable."

"Hmmm... how should I put it? Yes, at first it was awful. Even worse because I wasn't used to it, and my enemy, that Savakirey, was pretty skilled at striking my back so that it'd swell up without bleeding. But I developed a trick of my own – every time he smashed his whip down on me, I'd pull my skin up under the strike and tear it, and that way my back didn't swell up so insufferably, and I fixed that Savakirey the best he'd had it, fixed him so good it was the last flogging match of his life."

"'Fixed' him? Are you saying you beat him quite to death?"

"I am. You see, it was through his own thickness and his own stupid policy that he came to be erased from this earth," the storyteller answered genially, and without much emotion, and, seeing that his audience was staring back with, if not horror, then mute bewilderment, he felt he needed to flesh out his story with a little more detail.

"It wasn't me who started this all, it was him. He was

renowned across the sands of the Ryn as a premier fighter, and his pride in the title was so great that he wouldn't surrender for anything in the world. He tried to bear his suffering nobly – maybe he was afraid that he might dishonor the entire Asiatic race – but he just couldn't withstand what I gave him, the poor guy, especially because I had put a penny in my mouth. Helps an awful lot, that does, and I just bit down on it, to help with the pain, counting the lashes in my head, so that I barely noticed they kept landing on me."

Someone interrupted, "So how many blows did you count?"

"I probably couldn't tell you. I remember counting up to two hundred and eighty-two, when suddenly I felt a swoon coming on, just for a minute, and while I was fighting it off I lost count. But it didn't even matter, because just then Savakirey took his last flail at me – only he didn't even have the strength left to hit me, he just flopped forward toward me like a dropped puppet: you could see he was dead... oh, that's me alright! What an idiot. To think: *this* was what I'd been holding out for! Now I'd be lucky to keep myself out of jail. Now, Tatars, see – to them it's nothing at all: you killed him, you didn't kill him, all the same, and he'd have done the same to you. But over on our side, oh, those Russians! It drove me crazy, how dense they were, making such a fuss about it. So then I say, "Well, what's it to you? What do you want from me?"

"What do you mean," they reply. "We just saw you kill that Asiatic!"

"What if I did kill him? Call it a labor of love. You would've preferred, what, I let him do me in?"

"Why," they reply, "he could have done whatever he wanted with you, and we wouldn't care at all – he's a heathen! But you," they say, "you will be judged by Christian law. Come on, now – to the police station!"

I'm thinking to myself, *Alright, you fine set of pals – find a field and you want to put the wind on trial.* And since there's no one more perverted than the police, I ducked behind first one Tatar and then another, whispering to them, "Please save me, princes! You saw for yourselves how fair I fought…"

They pulled in tight in front of me and kept me hidden behind them. And then they really helped me disappear.

"Please, I don't understand. What do you mean, *disappear*?"

"I mean that I disappeared with them, to the steppe!"

"Really? The steppe?!"

"Oh, really – as far the very sands of the Ryn."

"And were you there long?"

"All of ten years: I was twenty-three when I disappeared into the Ryn sands, and thirty-four when I left for good."

"Did you find that you liked your life out in the steppe?"

"Like it? What is there to like!? It's sheer boredom, restless and homesick, and beyond that there's nothing. Just that it took me that long to make my escape."

"How come? Did they lock you up? Throw you in some pit?"

"No, they're kindly people, they would never have been so ungracious! No, no pit, no stocks. They would say, 'Be our friend, Ivan. We like you very much, live here on the steppe with us and help you out – take care of our horses when they're sick, and help our old ladies.'"

"And you did this?"

"I did. I worked among them as a healer, treating the men, and their cattle, and horses, and sheep, but most of all their ladies the Tataresses."

"Do you really know how to heal?"

"Well, how should I put this… for one thing, there's not much to it, is there? I'd just give them some aloe or galangal root. Good thing they had so much aloe – some Tatar had found a bagful over in Saratov and brought it back, and until I got there they never had a clue what to do with it."

"So you settled in among them?"

"Not really – I wanted out the whole time."

"There was really no way you could get away from them?"

"There wasn't. Maybe if my feet had been in better shape – then I would've sneaked out and made it back to my people a lot sooner."

"What was wrong with your feet?"

"I was all bristled up after my first attempt."

"What do you mean?… Excuse us, please, but we don't quite understand – what do you mean you were *bristled*?"

"It's the most ordinary thing in the world for them – if they start liking you and want to keep you around, and you're lonesome and melancholy and try to make an escape, they'll fix you up so you can never leave. That's what they did to me – I tried to cut myself loose, but I got lost once I left the road, and they caught me and said, 'You know, Ivan,' they said, 'we're making a friend of you, and so you can't get away from us again we're going to slice up your feet from the heel and shove some bristles in before we sew you back up.' Well, and believe me, that's just how they did it, screwed my feet up so bad I had to crawl around on all fours."

"Tell us, please, how was this monstrous surgery accomplished?"

"Very simply: ten of them pushed me to the ground and said, "You scream, Ivan, scream and scream louder while we start slicing in – helps with the pain." So they sat over me and one of them, a master at this foul craft, just sliced right away, and in no time at all they had shoved in some fine bristles clipped from a horse's mane, and then sewed me shut that way with some gut. After that, they kept me bound up for a few days, hand and foot, so that I didn't interfere with the wound's healing or soften up the bristles with pus. As the wound healed up, I was let free: 'Now,' they say, 'hi there, Ivan, now you are quite securely our friend and you'll never get away from us.'"

Just as soon as I got up on my feet, whoosh, down I went again, right back onto the ground: this chopped-up horsehair they'd stuck me with gave such a screaming pain as it dug into the living flesh on my foot that I couldn't take a single step, couldn't even figure out a way of standing on my feet. To that moment, I had never wept in my life. But oh, what wails I howled now, what howls I wailed!

"Why, what have you done to me, you godforsaken Asiatics?!" I say. "Better you vipers should have just annihilated me than forced me to live a hundred years as a cripple who can't even stand on his own two feet!"

And they say, "Ivan, Ivan, just listen to you, hollering emptily, all upset about nothing!"

"Nothing?! What do you mean, 'nothing'?! Is it nothing to cripple a man?! Why shouldn't I be upset?"

"Oh," they say, "you'll get used to it. You'll just have to walk around bow-legged. Try putting the weight on your anklebones."

"Damn you, you vile bastards!" I thought to myself and turned away from them without saying anything else. I made up my mind that I'd rather be dead than take their advice and walk around bowlegged on my anklebones. But later, while I was just lying around, a lonesome boredom as bad as death started creeping over me, and little by little I began to teach myself how to totter around on my ankles. That just made them laugh at me, and more than a little, and they'd even say, 'There you go, Ivan! That's good, look how well you can walk now.'"

"What a fate! What happened next? Did you escape and get caught again?"

"No, that was quite impossible. The steppe stretches out, flat and roadless, and a person's got to eat. Three days I walked, weaker and weaker. No worse than a fox, I caught some kind of a bird and ate it raw. But after I while I got hungry again, and there was no water to drink. Where to go? Finally I collapsed, and they came and found me and brought me back and bristled me up."

Someone from the audience observed that it must be a horrendous embarrassment, after the bristling, this way of walking around.

"When you're just starting out it's really pretty horrible." Ivan Severyanych answered, "but later on it gets easier, though I was never able to make it very far. But those Tatars, I'll tell you the truth, they started to take pity on me after that, and treated me awfully well.

"Now, Ivan," they'd say, "things are very hard for you – so uncomfortable that you can hardly get yourself any water or cook yourself any food. Here, brother, take a Natasha – pick a good one, we'll give you any Natasha you want."

"What's to choose from? They're all the same to me. Give me whatever one you want." Well, without any further discussion they up and married me off.

"What! So you were married to a Tataress?!"

"Yes of course she was a Tataress. Well, at first they married me off to the wife of Savarikey, that same one I'd flogged the life out of. But she wasn't my kind of woman at all: she wasn't quite right, always acting afraid of me. She didn't make me glad in the least. I think she missed her husband, maybe, or possibly something else was weighing on her heart. They noticed that I had started to burden her so they brought me another wife, this one just a girl, not older than thirteen. They said, "Here, Ivan, take this Natasha here, she'll show you a better time." So I did.

"And so? Did she in fact show you a better time?" one of the audience asked Ivan Severyanych.

"Oh, yes," he said, "we had more fun together. Sometimes she'd make me really glad, and then other times she'd spoil it by really getting to me."

"What'd she do to get to you?"

"Oh, different things... Whatever happened to occur to her. Like sometimes she'd jump on my knees; or maybe while I was sleeping she'd snatch the cap off my head with her foot, laughing her head off. You'd start to yell at her, and she'd just be cackling, running all around like some kind of rusalka, and you'd start chasing after her on all fours, but you could never catch up – and then you'd slip and fall over, and start cracking up yourself."

"So you shaved your head out there on the steppe, and started wearing a cap?"

"I did."

"How come? I guess you must have been trying to please your wives?"

"Not really – it's more out of a sense of hygiene. See, there's no baths out there."

"And you're saying you had two wives there at once?"

"Yes, on the steppe I had two. And later on, when I lived under Agashimola, a different Khan who had stolen me from Otuchev, he gave me two more."

"Pardon my interrupting," one of the audience jumped in, "but how could he steal you?"

"By pure skulduggery! There I was, having fled Penza with the Tatars of Chepkun Yemgurcheyev, and I lived five straight years among the Yemgurcheyevite horde. It was there that they all gathered in celebration, the princes and Uhlans and under-sheikhs and *their* under-sheikhs, even Djangar Khan and Bakshey Otuchev came."

"You mean the one Chepkun had beaten?"

"I do, the very same."

"But it doesn't make sense – wasn't Bakshey incensed at Chepkun?"

"Why would he be?"

"Why, for thrashing him and taking his horse!"

"Oh, not at all. You see, they never get mad at each other over such things. They're of a tender persuasion: someone wins and someone loses, and that's all there is to it. Although once Djangar Khan did give me kind of a hard time: 'Oh, Ivan,' he said, 'what a damned fool you are! To think that you sat and faced Savakirey right when that Russian prince himself was about to take up the challenge! I was ready for a good laugh, seeing that noble prince take off his shirt and get what's coming."

"You would've never seen it," I answer him, "no matter how long you'd waited."

"Why not?"

"Because our princes are lily-livered weaklings, not real men. Their strength is nothing to boast about."

He understood. "Yes, I could see there were no real sportsmen among them. Whatever they want they expect to buy with money."

"You said it: can't do a thing without their purses handy." But Agashimola, he was from the farthest horde, and his flocks grazed up north of the Caspian. He liked to do a bit of healing himself, and he asked me to come see if I could help his wife, promising the Yemgurcheyevites ample head of cattle to let me go. Yemgurcheyev agreed, so I gathered up my aloe and galangal roots and set out with him. But once he'd taken me, Agashimola galloped off with me and the rest of his tribe, eight days' journey across the steppe."

"So you went on horseback?"

"Yes, on horseback."

"And what about your feet?"

"How do you mean?"

"Well, the chopped-up horsehair inserted into your heels – wasn't it bothering you?"

"Not really. They've got it down to an art: they bristle you up at the heels so that you can't walk, but the process makes you a better rider than ever, because you're already used to holding your legs out crooked from all the bow-legged walking you've got to do. Soon you realize that you're able to clasp the horse between your legs like a hoop, and there isn't a horse that can throw you."

"So what happened to you on this new steppe with Agashimola?"

"Even crueler indignities were heaped upon me, bringing me closer to death than ever."

"Yet you didn't die?"

"No, of course not."

"Well, favor us, please, tell us what further travails you suffered under Agashimola."

"I'd be glad to."

VII

As soon as Agashimola's Tatars got me back home, they broke camp to look for a new place to stay and would not let me leave.

"Ivan," they said to me, "why would you want to go back and live with Yemgurcheyev? Yemgurcheyev's a thief. You live here with us, we'll bring you out hunting with us and give you great Natashas. There you had only two Natashas, but we'll make sure you have more."

I refused. "Why would I want more? Two is plenty."

"No," they replied, "you don't understand. The more Natashas, the better: they make you more Kolyas who scream and call you 'daddy.'"

"I don't take too lightly the prospect of raising up a whole crop of squealing Tatars. If I could baptize them properly and administer the sacraments, that'd be another story, but I can't: however many I had, they'd be you, not us. They'd never be Orthodox and might even grow up to cheat hardworking Russians." So I limited my new wives to two, because when there are too many women in a house, even Tatar women, they get to fussing and fighting, and I'd be constantly having to break up the spats.

"Well, so tell us, did you love these two new wives of yours?"

"How do you mean?"

"These new wives of yours, did you love them?"

"Love them?... If you're asking, well, what I *think* you're asking – there was one that I took from Agashimola who was constantly trying to appease me. I felt sorry for her."

"But the other girl, that young one you were talking about, you must have liked her too?"

"Fair enough. I found her sympathetic."

"Did you miss her, then, when you were off living with this new horde?"

"No, I didn't waste much time missing her."

"But look here, you must have had some children from those earlier marriages, mustn't you?"

"Well, of course. Savakirey's wife bore me two little Kolyas and a Natashka, and the other one, the young one, was able to bear me six in five years, since two of them were twins."

"Might I ask why you keep calling them 'Kolyas' and 'Natashkas'?"

"That's what they call us. Among Tatars, any grown Russian man is an Ivan, and a woman is a Natasha, and a little boy is a Kolya. And because of me, they considered my wives to be Russian, and so they called them Natashas and our sons Kolyas. I'm calling them my children, of course, only superficially; they never received the sacraments of the church, so they're no sons of mine."

"You don't consider them your own children?

"They can't be my children because they've never been baptized or anointed with myrrh."

"You have no parental feelings toward them?"

"How do you mean?"

"Didn't you love these children just a little? Didn't you ever want to hold them close and caress them?"

"Caress them? Sometimes I'd be sitting alone and one of them would run over and, sure, I'd pat him gently on the head and say, 'Go to your mother.' But this didn't happen very often, because I didn't really have the time for it."

"Didn't have time? Why not? Did you have a great deal of business to attend to?"

"No, I had no business of any kind. But I was lonesome, melancholy. I wanted so badly to return home to Russia."

"And so for ten years you never left the steppe?"

"Not once. Oh, how I longed to go home! The sadness of it was overwhelming. Especially in the evenings, or in the middle of the day when the weather was fine, hot enough to cook an egg, and it was quiet in the camp, since when it's hot all the Tatars clamber into their yurts to nap, and I would lift up the flap in front of my tent and stare out at the steppe… from one end to the other, all exactly the same… a simmering landscape, and cruel. Endless space without boundaries; grass, in its complete savagery; white mat grass, downy, billowing like a silvery sea, scenting the breeze with a smell of sheep; and the sun steaming down, sizzling, and the steppe as endlessly burdensome as life is, no end anywhere in sight, and no bottom to my sadness... you look out from there never knowing what you're seeing, and suddenly you'd spot some monastery or chapel, and remember your own Christian land and start bawling."

Ivan Severyanych fell silent for a minute, sighed heavily with all he was remembering, and went on.

"It was even worse out among the salt marshes by the Caspian: that sun glaring, baking, and both the shimmering saltwater and the sea itself shimmering... the mad brilliance of this was even more disorienting than the light off the mat grass and would leave you unable to say where you were, in what part of the world, alive or dead or even in hell suffering endless punishment for your sins. There, where the steppe is downy with mat grass, the landscape is a little less grim, at least; out there from time to time you'll see a bush of sage growing, or a soft little mugwort or some thyme to fleck the endless spaces with green. In the marshes there's nothing but that endless shimmer. Sometimes someone would start a fire, and let it blaze across the grass, raising a giant, swirling to-do, great and little bustards circling all around, and steppe snipes, and we'd have a little fun hunting them down. The great bustards we'd chase down on horses and smash with our long whips, until our horses too had to run and escape from the advancing flames. This was all of our favorite game. And then soon afterward the old field would open into a bloom of wild strawberries; birds, all different birds but mostly the littler ones, would alight and swell the air with songs. From time to time you'd come upon something else: some meadowsweet growing, or little wild peaches, or wormwood, and when the sun came up and mist fell and became dew, the air would get a sweet waft of resins… even then, you'd find it lonesome and dull there, and God keep any man from being forced to spend much time in those salt marshes! For a horse, though, it's not a bad deal: he licks salt all day, and then drinks a ton of water and gets fat. For a man, it's certain doom. In fact, there's no wildlife there of any kind, except, and this is worth a laugh, a certain little bird, the redpoll, a little like the swallows we have, a most unremarkable animal, except perhaps for a red fringe on its beak that looks like a lip. Why they flock to these shores I don't know, but since there's nothing for them to land and rest on, they just plop right down on the marshland itself, lie down on their little rumps for a minute and, while you watch, take to the air again and fly. You don't get to join, since you have no wings, so you just sit there and watch, and there's no death, and no life, and no penance you can do, and you'll die there and soak in the brine like mutton, pickling until the end of time like a piece of salt meat. Even worse is to spend a winter in these wastes: not much snow, just enough to cover the grass and solidify – and the Tatars just sit around the fires in their yurts, smoking… and things often get so dull that they just decide to go at it and flog each other from boredom. If you step outside, there's nothing to look at: the horses grow spindly and wander around, their ribs showing through, their manes and tails waving limply in the breeze. They can barely scrape their hooves across the ground, and they swallow the snow for water and the frozen grass for the only fodder they'll get. Just unbearable. The only break comes when you spot a horse so weak that he can't scrape through the snow or get any frozen grass into his mouth – then they'll jab a knife in his throat and skin his body for meat. The meat, though, is just putrid: sweet, like a cow's udder, but tough. You endure eating this, of course, but only because you have to. One of my wives, thankfully, knew how to smoke a horse's rib meat: you take the rib just as though you were going to eat it, with meat hanging off on both sides, and then you stuff it like a sausage into a big gut, and smoke it over the hearth. This wasn't *quite* as bad – at least the flavor reminded you of smoked ham a little – but it was revolting all the same. I'd be chewing on that foul crap and suddenly I'd think: 'oh, back home in the village they're preparing for Christmas, plucking the geese, slaughtering the pigs, cooking up pots of schi with neckbones, oh, such fat little neckbones!' And Father Ilya, our priest, a little old man as kind as kind can be, he'd be leading the procession to the glory of Christ, the deacons with him, and the priests' wives and deacons' wives, seminary students too, all of them drunk, though Father Ilya himself can't hold much: in the manor house a butler would offer him a little glass of something; at the offices the overseer would send a nurse out with another, Father Ilya crawling and dragging himself to the servant's quarters, drunk as anything, scraping his feet. In the first cottage from the edge of town he'd somehow end up drinking another glass, but after that he really couldn't get more down, and he'd just empty everything into a bottle he kept under his chasuble. Plus, being so devoted to family life, even where food was concerned, if he caught sight of any uneaten morsel he'd say, 'Wrap that up in some newspaper, I'll take it with me.' More often than not they'd reply, 'But Father, we haven't got any newspaper,'" and he never got mad, he'd just grab it in whatever state it was in, hand it like that to his wife, and keep moving on in absolute peace… oh, my friends, when those childhood memories stirred and welled up inside me, and pressed on my heart, and suddenly started churning in my liver, I'd say to myself, 'Look where you've ended up, so endlessly distant from all that happiness, so far from spiritual comfort for all these years, living unwed and bound to die unmourned, endless sorrows overwhelming you…' then I'd steal out silently into the night, where no wife and no children and no damned heathens had any chance of spotting me, and there'd I'd start to pray… I'd pray and pray and not even notice that the snow had melted under my knees and that I could see the grass now where my tears had been falling."

The storyteller paused and bowed his head. Nobody bothered him; it seemed that everyone wanted to respect the sacred suffering of his memories. But after a minute had passed, Ivan Severyanych let out a heavy sigh and gave a wave of his hand. He took the novice's cap from his head and, crossing himself, said, "Well, thanks be to God, it all passed eventually."

After giving him a minute to catch his breath, we felt emboldened to ask more questions about how he, our enchanted bogatyr, had managed to free his feet of the bristles that bound them and escape the Tatar steppe and those Natashas and Kolyas, and how he had wound up in a monastery.

Ivan Severyanych satisfied our curiosity, displaying that absolute forthrightness he clearly had no talent for avoiding.

VIII

Holding crucial as we did the exact sequencing of the events in developing the story of Ivan Severyanych, we asked him to tell us to what extraordinary lengths he'd had to go to free himself of those bristles and flee his captivity. He obliged us exactly, and this is the story he told:

I had completely despaired of ever returning home and seeing my beloved motherland. The idea seemed totally out of the question now, and gradually even my homesickness and melancholy began to die down. I went around unfeeling as a statue, and that was that. But sometimes I'd get to thinking about Father Ilya back home, the one who was always asking for a newspaper, and how during the service he'd always offer a prayer "for all who journey by water and air, those who suffer, those held captive." In church I always used to think to myself: "*How come*? Is there some war on somewhere, that we should be praying for prisoners?" But now at last I could understand why we had always prayed for them – what I couldn't understand was why all the prayers were coming to nothing for me now, and, to make a long story short, I'm no unbeliever, but, I dithered, and I stopped praying altogether.

"What's the use praying," I thought, "when nothing ever comes of it?"

One day, in the middle of everything, my ears pick up on something: all Tatardom in an uproar. I say, "What's going on?"

"Oh, nothing," they tell me. "Two mullahs have arrived from your country, under an emblem of safe conduct from the White Tsar, on a mission of spreading their faith far and wide."

I run over. "Where are they?"

They pointed to a yurt and I went where they pointed, I went and in I looked: a large gathering of under-sheikhs and sub-mullahs, and imams and dervishes, all sitting on rugs, and among them two strangers who, even though they were dressed for travel, you could tell were of the cloth. They were sitting in the middle of this mob and teaching all Tatardom the Word of God.

As soon as I caught sight of them and saw they were Russian, my heart leapt up in my chest and I fell sobbing at their feet.

They rejoiced at my prostration and both cried out, "And so, and so, do you see? Do you see! Look how God's grace does wonders! It has but touched one of your brethren, and he turns his back on Mohammed!"

The Tatars replied that there was nothing to behold: This is an Ivan, one of yours, of the Russians, he just lives with us here as our prisoner.

This displeased the missionaries immensely. They didn't believe I was a Russian, so I piped up myself. "No," I said, "I'm Russian as they come! Spiritual Fathers, have mercy on me, get me out of here! I've been a prisoner here for ten years, and you can see for yourself how they've crippled me: I can't walk!"

But they paid not a moment's heed and turned their backs on me, and what do you know, went right on preaching!

I thought to myself, "What's the point of grumbling? They're here on official business, maybe they'd find it compromising to offer me special treatment in front of the Tatars." So I let it alone for a while, and waited till they were alone in the guest tent, and then I snuck over and gave them my whole story in all sincerity, the harrowing fate that had claimed me, and I asked them: "Oh, blessed Fathers, please, put the fear of our papa the White Tsar into them! Tell them he doesn't want Asiatics holding his subjects captive, no, no, better yet, give them some ransom for me, and when I'm free from here I'll work in your service. I've been living with them and I've learned their language like a native: I could be awfully useful to you."

"Oh, son," they said, "we have no ransom to offer, and we are under strict orders not to offend the heathens, since, though they be a cunning and faithless mob, we must maintain decorum in the interest of politics."

"Are you saying," I said, "that I have to spend my whole life here with them for your precious politics?"

"It matters little where a man spends his life," they said.

"Pray, son. God's ways are full of kindness. Perhaps he will deliver you."

"I've prayed, believe me, I've prayed, but I'm out of strength and I'm losing hope!"

"Do not despair," they said. "For that is a great sin!"

"I'm not despairing! It's just... what a shameful way for you to treat me, me a compatriot and fellow Russian! I can't believe you won't lend a hand."

"No, child," they answered, "do not try to involve us in such matters. We are joined in Christ, and in Christ there is neither Gentile nor Jew; all of our countryfolk obey God's law. In our eyes all men are equal, all equal."

"All?" I say.

"Yes," they reply, "all. This is our learning from the Apostle Paul. Wherever we go, we avoid making trouble. It is not in our interest. You are but a servant to the Almighty, and what must you do? You must be patient, for as the Apostle Paul has written, the task of a servant is to serve. Remember that you are a Christian, and so we have no business with you, for to you the gates of Heaven are already open. But these men here will remain in darkness if we do not come to preach among them, and so it is with them that we must deal."

And they took out a little ledger book. "Look here," they say, "do you see how many names are written in this register? These are all the men we have brought over to the true faith!"

I didn't waste another word on them, and never saw them again either, except once. What happened was that one of my little boys came running up and said, "Daddy, daddy, there's a man lying in the lake over there!"

I went over to take a look. I could see they had stripped the socks from his feet and the gloves from his hands. The Tatars have this all worked out: they slice in a ring around the arm or the leg, and the skin can be peeled right off. The man's head was lying not far away, with a cross carved into it.

"Oh, countryman – you didn't want to do a thing for me, and I cursed you. Now look, you've been made a martyr, worthy of the crown of suffering. Please forgive me, I beg you, for Christ's sake!"

I made a cross over him, laid his head next to the rest of him, prostrated myself to the ground, and then buried him, saying an "Our Father" over the grave. What happened to his companion I never managed to find out, but I think he must've met a similar end, because afterward all the women of the horde were passing around devotional knickknacks, making little toys of them, the same ones the missionaries had brought with them.

"Is it common for missionaries to go so far as the sands of the Ryn?" Ivan Severyanych was asked.

"They go sometimes, but it never comes to anything."

"Why not?"

"Dealing with them – they just don't know how. An Asiatic responds only to fear, you must convert him with such fear that it makes him tremble, and yet they preach a God of humble resignation. So it comes to nothing, because nothing will make an Asiatic respect a God without vengefulness, and instead they just murder his preachers!"

"So in preaching to these Asiatics, a man had better not have any money or jewels with him!"

"No, he'd better not. But even so, they can't imagine that anyone would come through empty-handed, they'll just assume that he's got it buried somewhere across the steppe, and start digging and digging for it."

"The ruffians!"

"They sure are. I'll give you another example, something I saw them do to a Jew once. This Jew just showed up one day, and he too started to profess his faith. A good man, and, it seemed, true to his beliefs, dressed in such tatters that you could see the naked flesh right through his clothes. And he preached with such fire that I wished his sermons could go on forever. Well, when he started I was ready to quarrel, demanding to know how he could account for a faith like this one, with no saints at all! But then he told me that it *does* have saints, and he began reading aloud from the Talmud all about the different saints there were, and it was so terribly interesting, this Talmud, which, he told me, had been written by a certain Rabbi Jovoz Ben Levi, said to be so learned that the sinful couldn't even bear to look at him, since as soon as they did they'd be struck dead, which was why the Almighty Himself had called upon him to say, 'Listen, you learned Rabbi, Jovoz Ben Levi! It is good that you are so wise, but it is not good that you have the power to fell all my little Jews dead. It wasn't for this that I led them with Moses across the desert and over the sea.

Go, then, find a place outside your homeland where you can live without anybody ever seeing you.' And Rabbi Levi went and wandered off and around until he reached the very place where Paradise had been, and there he buried himself in sand up to his neck and stayed that way for thirteen years, and every Saturday he prepared himself a feast of lamb roasted in a fire that descended down from Heaven. And anytime a mosquito or fly would perch on his nose to sip at his blood, it too would be instantly roasted in celestial fire… the Asiatics delighted in this story, and spent a long, long time listening to the little old Jew, but after a while they started peppering him with unrelated questions: Where had he buried his money, before he got here? The little Jewish papa swore that he had no money, that God had sent him wandering with nothing in the world but wisdom to his name, but they didn't believe him. And they grabbed a coal out of the fire, and wrapped it in horse hide, and began to shake it over him. Tell us, they said: Where's the money? And then they saw that he'd gone black all over, and his screams had died down: 'Hey, let's bury him in the sand up to his neck – maybe that'll bring him around!' And they did, and so the poor Jew died like that. For a long time after they just left his blackened head poking out of the sand. After a while the children got afraid of it, and so they cut it down and tossed it into a dry old well."

"So that's what you get for preaching to them!"

"Yes – just terrible. Though in this case, you know, it turns out that Jew had some money after all."

"He did?!"

"Oh, he did. Once the wolves and the jackals started fussing with him, they dragged him out from his hole and tore him apart all over the sand. When they got to his boots and started pulling them apart, seven silver coins fell out. They were found later."

"How did you manage to escape from them?"

"I was saved by a miracle."

"Who worked this miracle for you?"

"Talafa."

"Who is this Talafa? Another Tatar?'

"No, he's of quite a different race. He's Indian, and not just an Indian, but an Indian god who came to earth."

Giving in to the entreaties of his listeners, Ivan Severyanych Flyagin had the following to say about this new chapter in the ongoing tragicomedy of his life.

IX

When winter came again, when it had been about a year since the Tatar's disposal of the missionaries, we drove our herds south to graze in a new spot, closer to the Caspian, and here, one day just before evening, two men appeared in camp – if you could even call them men. Who knew *what* they were, from what region and what nation? They had no true tongue, speaking neither Russian nor Tatar, but rather a word here or there of each, and to each other they spoke some God-knows-what barbarous lingo. Neither of them was past middle age, one black with a great beard and a robe not too different from a Tatar robe, except all red, while theirs are dotted in different colors, and on his head a pointed Persian hat. The other one, a redhead, also wore a long robe, but he seemed to be more of a troublemaker: he had with him boxes, all sorts of boxes, and whenever he had a minute's privacy he'd take the robe off and walk around in little breeches and a coat, the kind of outfit German factory workers used to wear in Russia in the old days. Whatever was in those boxes he couldn't stop touching and toying with it; what it was only he himself knew. It was said that they had come from Khiva to procure horses, for a war that maybe they were stirring up with someone back home, or something like that – they never made it clear, but instead spent their time working up anti-Russian resentment in the Tatars. I heard that the redheaded one, he couldn't talk much, and every time he tried to get his mouth around the word *adminis-chraytor*, he'd spit. But they didn't have any money with them, since, being Asiatics themselves, they knew that riding out onto the steppe with cash you took your life in your hands. They were trying to get the Tatars to agree to drive their flocks down to the River Syr Darya and finish their business there. The Tatars were all over the map, and they couldn't agree whether or not to accept the offer. They thought and thought and thought about it, so deliberately that you'd think they were prospecting for gold, and you could tell there was something they were afraid of.

The two of them began by trying to use their honor to persuade the Tatars; this strategy soon gave way to fear. "You'd better get racing," they said, "or things will get ugly here. We have a God called Talafa, and he sent his fire here with us. We hope he does not get angry."

The Tatars had never heard of this god, and they doubted he'd bring his fire down on them in the steppe in the middle of winter. But this blackbeard, who had come from Khiva in a flowing red robe, just said, if you doubt us, then Talafa will make a demonstration of his terrible strength in the night. "But I warn you," he says, "no matter what you see or hear, do not run out from your tents, or he'll burn you to a cinder." Of course, in all the steppe's winter boredom, we got pretty excited for the distraction, even though we were a little afraid to see what was going to come out of this Indian god – who would he turn out to be, by what wonders would he reveal himself?

We went back into our tents early, our wives and our children with us, and waited. It was all very dark and silent, a night like any, and then suddenly, just as I had been drifting off, I heard a high wheezing wind that exploded overhead with a sudden thunder, and through my sleep it looked to me as if a thousand sparks were drifting downward from the heavens.

I shook myself, glanced around, saw my wives were jittering around and my kids starting to cry.

"Hush! Plug their mouths, shut them up!"

They started nursing and things began to quiet down again, and then suddenly another fire hissed across the steppe sky, hissed and again exploded with a crash.

"I think, I think I'd say – this Talafa, he's no joke!"

After a little while, he started hissing again, but this time in a different way – like a bird made of flame, he fluttered his tail, also of flame, and the flame was remarkable: red, as red as blood, and then a burst, and suddenly everything becomes yellow and then blue.

Everything in the camp, I noticed, had grown silent as a grave. Of course, no one could have missed hearing such a ruckus, which meant that everyone was lying low under their sheepskins. All you could hear was the earth every so often giving a tremor, and then quieting down again. This, you could figure, must have been the horses cowering and huddling together in heap. Then I heard those Khivans or Indians or whatever they were running somewhere, and then another fire thundering over the steppe like a dragon. The horses let out a squeal and bolted. The Tatars forgot their fear completely and ran out, shaking their heads around, bellowing "Allah! Allah!" And as for those Khivans, they just up and disappeared without a trace, except a single one of those boxes to remember them by. All of the strong men were out chasing the herd, and leaving me behind with just the women and old men, and so I got to wondering: "What's in that box?" I peeked inside: various earths, and elixirs, and paper tubes. I held one of these tubes too close to the fire, and it burst into flame, almost took my eye out, and soared into the sky, where... *ppppoooowwww*, and it scattered into a little drizzle of stars. "Aha!" I thought to myself. "It's no god at all! Just regular fireworks, like we used to set off in the park." I decided to set off another one, for the old ladies, and what do you know, the old men who'd stayed behind all fell on their faces and lay where they'd landed, wiggling their legs. At first I almost got afraid too, but I saw that they were just lying there flopping, and for the first time since I'd been there I started grinding my teeth and intoning a string of meaningless words as loud as I could: "parlay-bien-com-sa-shiray-meer-ferfkyukhtur-min-adieu-m'sieu!"

I set off another, a Catherine wheel. When they saw

that thing trailing fire, I thought the fear might kill them! The fire went out, and they all lay there, face-down like before, and one of them beckoned me over with his finger. I came up to him and said, "What'll it be, you damned foul thing! Life or death?!" because I could see they were terrified of me.

"We're sorry, Ivan," they say. "Please, let us live!"

From all around they started waving me over one after another, just to beg me to forgive them and spare their lives. I could see things were taking a pretty good turn for me at last; it must have been that everything I'd endured had finally atoned for my sins, so I prayed: "Most Holy Mother of God, Saint Nicholas, please, help me, my darlings, my saviors!"

In a strict voice I asked one of the Tatars, "For what sins do you apologize? To what purpose do you ask me to spare your lives?"

"We apologize," they said, "for not believing in your god."

"Aha," I think, "so that's how afraid they are!" And I say, "I'm afraid not, oh brothers. I can never forgive your hostility to my religion!" I started grinding my teeth again and lit up another one of the tubes.

This time it was a rocket… a boom and a terrifying crash of flame.

I scream at the Tatars, "This is it: just one more minute and I'll destroy every last one of you, if you don't put your faith in my god!"

"Don't kill us," they answer, "we'll submit to your god!"

So I stopped the fireworks and baptized them in a little stream nearby.

"You're saying you baptized them that very same day?"

"The very same minute! What would be the point of killing time? I didn't want them to have a chance to change their minds. I sprinkled their heads with water over an ice-hole, said In the name of the Father and of the Son, put crosses around their necks left behind by the missionaries. I told them to venerate the missionaries as martyrs, and showed them where their graves were."

"And they prayed?"

"They did."

"But they must not have known any Christian prayers, or did you teach them some?"

"There was no time for that – I could see it was my time to escape. I just told them to pray the way they always had, but don't you dare call on Allah, instead always remember to substitute the name of Jesus Christ. This procedure they accepted."

"But, so how did you manage to get away from these new Christians with your feet all bristled up and how did you manage to fix them?"

"Inside the fireworks kit, I found a caustic kind of an earth, so that if even a dab touches the skin, it starts to heat up and blister something awful. I grabbed it and starting playing sick, and then while I was lying under the rug I applied it to my heels, and for two weeks I kept putting more on, so that my feet got completely covered with blistering sores, and then all that hair the Tatars had shoved in there ten years earlier was flushed out with the pus. I healed up as quickly as I could, but I pretended to be getting even worse, and even asked the women and the old men to pray for me as hard as they could, because, it seemed, I was dying. I laid a kind of a penance on them, ordering them to fast and stay inside their yurts for three days, and then I let off the biggest firework in the box to scare them good, and I left."

"They never caught you?"

"No, they couldn't – I'd scared them so well and left them so weak from all the fasting that they were quite eager not to stick their noses out for three days, and by then I was too far gone for them to catch me. With the bristles out, my feet had healed up completely, and they had become so light that no sooner had I started to run than I had run from one end of the steppe to the other."

"This is all oer grass?"

"How else! No sir, there's no beaten track out there and certainly no roads. You never see anyone else, and if you do you're not always so glad for the company. On the fourth day I came across a Chuvash tribesman, one man driving five horses, and he said to me, 'Hey, hop on.' I thought about it for a minute and decided not to."

"What were you afraid of?"

"He just didn't look right to me, I guess, and it was impossible to make out his religion. In the steppe you're never safe without knowing that. But like an idiot, he just keeps shouting, "Hey, get on, more fun ride two together!"

"Who are you? For all I know you don't even have a god!"

"Vat?" he says. "No, ish Tatar have no god, he eat horshesh! But I hash god."

"Well, tell me," I say, "who your god is."

"To me," he replied, "ish all god: shun ish god, moon ish god, shtarsh ish god, everything god! Vat you mean me no got god?"

"Everything! Hm, everything is your god. So is Jesus Christ your god too?"

"Oh yesh," he said, "he god too, and bleshed mother god, and shaint Nicholash god…"

"Which Nicholash?"

"The vone live in vinter and the vone live in shummer."

I congratulated him on his respect for the Russian Saint Nicholas, Worker of Miracles.

"Always honor him," I said, "because he is Russian." I was about to tell the tribesman that I thought he was alright and I'd go along with him after all, but, thank goodness, I waited another a minute and his true colors came out.

"Oh yesh," he said, "I honor Nicholash. I no kneel to him in the vinter, no, but in shummer I alvays give him twenty kopecks sho he look after my cowsh. But I alsho pray to another, I shlaughter calf to Keremetee!"

I was infuriated.

"How dare you not place all your faith in Saint Nicholas the Worker of Miracles! How can you only give him, a Russian, twenty kopecks, while you offer a whole bull to vile Keremetee! Be on your way – I can't, I won't ride with someone who has so little respect for Nicholas the Worker of Miracles!"

So I didn't go with him: I strode away at full steam, and scarcely had I had time to get myself together before what do I see, toward the evening of my third day out, but water up ahead, and some people. I dove into the grass for cover and watched them for a while. What kind of people were these? You see I was afraid I might end up in some even worse confinement, but when I saw what they were up to – cooking a meal! I thought to myself, "They must be Christians!" I crawled a little closer and I could see that they were crossing themselves and drinking vodka – obvious Russians! I leapt out of the grass and let them see me. It turned out they were a group of fishermen, there with the day's catch. They received me warmly as countrymen should, and hollered, "Drink vodka with us!"

I answered, "My brothers, I'm quite unused to drink, having been living among Tatars for some time."

"So what," they said, "you're back with your own kind now, so you'd better get used to it again: drink up!"

I poured myself a glass and thought, "Well, thanks be to God, here's to coming home!" and I drank it right down, but the fishermen – what a bunch of guys they were! – insisted I have another.

"Another drink!" they shouted, "see how weak you've grown away from it!"

One more drink and I became pretty affable. I mean I told them everything, where I'd come from and where I'd been, how I'd gotten by. All night I sat with them by the fire, telling my sad story, drinking vodka, and my spirits were so high to be home in Holy Russia, but in the morning, when the fire had gone out and almost the whole crew had fallen asleep, one of the team of fishermen said to me, "So, you got papers?"

"Nope, nothing."

"But if you haven't got them," he said, "they'll throw you in jail back home."

"I guess that means I'll have to stick around. A guy could live with you fishermen without papers, couldn't he?"

"Well, sure, a guy could *live* here without papers. What he couldn't do is die."

"Why is that?"

"Well," he explained, "how's the priest supposed to register your death, if you haven't got papers?"

"What would happen to me then?"

"You," he replied, "we would throw in the river to be fish food."

"Without a priest?"

"Without a priest."

Being a little drunk, I got so terribly afraid about this that I started to weep and moan, and the fisherman laughed at me.

"I was just pulling your leg," he said. "Die with confidence! We'll bury you right in the good old earth of Mother Russia."

But I was incensed and said, "Some joke! Keep them coming like that one and I won't live to springtime!"

As soon as this last fisherman had fallen asleep, I slipped off and walked away, and after a while I got to Astrakhan, where I found work as a journeyman for a ruble a day and took to drink. I drank so hard that I can't even remember how I ended up in the next city, rotting in jail there no less, and from there I was sent back under guard to my home province. They brought me into town, thrashed me pretty good down at the police station, and then sent me back to the old estate. The Countess, the same one who'd had me whipped over the cat's tail, had already died, and only the Count now remained, but he had aged terribly and become terribly devout, given up hunting on horseback altogether. They announced my arrival to him, and he remembered me and announced that I should be flogged again immediately and then taken before little Father Ilya for confession. They whipped me just like in the good old days, over in the records office, and then I went before Father Ilya, and he listened to everything and refused to grant me absolution for another three years.

I said, "What should I do in the meantime, Dear Father? It's been so many years since I've taken the sacrament… I thought after waiting so long…"

"It hardly matters how long you've waited," he said. "Can you tell me why you've kept Tatar women as wives? Have you any idea what a mercy I've done you? If I handled this by the official rules of the church as set down by our Holy Fathers, I would have set you on fire and let your clothes burn off. But don't you worry about that; that's become a violation of the penal code."

"Well," I thought, "what is there to do? I'll just have to return home without the sacrament, and spend some time around the house, healing from my captivity." But the Count didn't want it that way. He was gracious enough to say, "I will not allow a man excommunicated by the church to live near me."

So he had the groundskeeper beat me again as a public example and then he let me go, free so long as I paid him an annual tax. They beat me in a new way this time, on the stairs in front of the manor's main office, in front of everybody, and they gave me a passport. After so many years, I was overjoyed to be a free man once again, with legal papers no less, and I headed off. I didn't have any next move in mind, but God soon put me to work.

"What sort of work?"

"The same as before: work with horses. I started out with absolutely nothing, penniless, but soon I was making enough to get by. I soon had the opportunity to try for something even better, and I could have, if not for just one thing."

"And what was that, if you don't mind my asking?"

"I became possessed by a whole menagerie of spirits and ghouls, and also by one other little inconvenience."

"What 'little inconvenience' could you mean?"

"Magnetism."

"What? Magnetism?"

"Yes, One man's magnetic influence."

"How would this influence be felt?"

"A strange man's will surged through me, and I fulfilled a strange man's fate."

"So this was when your own ruin finally came to you, after which you found that you had to fulfill the promise of your mother and took your vows at the monastery?"

"No, that all came later. I still had many adventures in store before that day would dawn when I heard my true calling."

"Could you tell us about these adventures?"

"Why, of course I could. With the greatest of pleasure."

"Well then, please."

X

Papers in hand I drifted on, no particular idea of where to go, and I came upon a fair, where I saw a gypsy trading horses with a simple Russian peasant. The gypsy was cheating him brazenly. To show off the horse's strength he'd hitched it to a cartload of millet, while the Russian's was hitched to a cart of apples, so that it looked even but wasn't, and the peasant's horse was sweating from the stink of apples, which horses can't stand, and besides I could see he was a fainter from a small insignia branded into his lip, which the Gypsy tried to wave away with a quick "That? Oh, that's a wart." Naturally I felt sorry for the little peasant, who'd never be able to put this fainting horse to work for him, since it might keel over any second. Besides, I'd come round to a deathly hatred of gypsies, since it was a gypsy who first tempted me into my life of wandering and sadness, and there must have been something else I felt too, some twinge of a premonition, which turned out to be justified. I unmasked the gypsy's ruse before the peasant, and when the gypsy had the nerve to insist it wasn't a brand on the horse's lip but a wart, I proved my point by jabbing his horse in the kidney with an awl, so that it fell on the ground and went into a seizure. I went and used my judgment – which, you remember, was very refined where horses are concerned – and I found him a good one. they were all so grateful that they treated me to wine and a little picnic, and gave me twenty hryvnias. We all had a great time together, celebrating. That's pretty much how it happened: my capital began growing, and my love of drink kept pace, til hardly a month had gone by before I found myself on the up and up. I decked myself out in silver plates and a harness and went around from fair to fair, where I'd always take the poor peasants by the hand and help them out, and if they wanted to show their thanks with a fee? Terrific. A fee and a drink? Even better. In the meantime I was like a bolt of divine vengeance against all the gypsy hucksters, and I caught wind of a rumor that they were cooking up a beating for me. There being so many of them, and just one of me, I got, let's say, a little shy, and didn't hang around them much, so that there was never a time when one of them could get the drop on me. They wouldn't dare lay a finger on me in front of the peasants, who were all grateful for my virtue and stood up for me no matter what. So instead, they cooked up a vile rumor that I was a warlock, and that all my power with horses came straight from the Devil. But of course that went nowhere, since I'm willing to tell anyone the secret of my natural gift for horses, even though it won't get them anywhere.

"Won't get them anywhere? Why not?"

"No one can truly grasp it but me. You've got to be born with such a gift! I've tried teaching it to more than a few pupils, always in vain. Indulge me, gentlemen, and I'll tell you that whole story too."

Soon my name echoed across the empire from one fair to the next, and one day a purchaser for the cavalry, a prince, handed me a hundred rubles and said, "C'mon, brother, let me in on your secret. It'd be worth a lot to me, and I'd make it worth your while, too."

"Ah, but I have no secret!" I said. "It's simply a gift I was born with."

He stayed at it, "Then just tell me how you do it, whatever it takes, and just so you know I mean business, here, have another hundred."

What to do? I gave a shrug, put the money in my satchel, and said, "Sir, I'll glad teach you everything I know, if you'll oblige me to listen carefully. But let me be clear: if I teach you everything and you get nothing out of it, that won't be my fault."

But strangely, he found this agreeable, and said, "Never you worry about what I can learn, just start teaching!"

"First things first," I say. "When you're inspecting a horse, you have to look him over real close, put in the very closest inspection – there's no getting around that. You start by examining the head, and put a lot of thought into it, and then you can move backwards down the whole length of the horse to his tail, and don't get your paws all over him the way cavalry officers always do. They always begin by feeling up a horse's crest, then forelock, and then its windpipe and breast, and all for nothing. That's what horse traders love so much about cavalry officers: as soon as they see one running his mitts along some horse, they'll start turning him around, not letting him still for a second, so that any blemish they want to conceal is always on the far side – an incredibly common con, and that's how it works. If a horse holds one ear higher than the other, they'll clip a scrap of flesh from the back of his neck, pull tight what's left and sew it up, slather the wound with ointment, and that evens them out. But not for long – soon the skin loosens up and the ear starts sagging again. Or if the ears are too big, they'll clip them to size and stand them up with little shards of horn. If someone wants to buy a team of two horses, and, let's say, only one of them has a star on his forehead, these shysters will go to any length to give a star to the other one: they'll rub its fur with pumice, or apply a turnip hot from the oven wherever they want white hairs to grow, and it works, but if you examine a horse like that closely enough you'll see that the hairs are longer there, and they curl around his face like whiskers. Their tricks with a horse's eyes are even more outrageous: some horses have little blemishes above their eyes, real ugly ones, and so the dealer will poke him there with a pin, get his lips around the hole, and blow and blow as hard as he can until the skin pulls tight and refreshes the natural beauty of the eye. It's pretty easy because horses like the feel of your breath, how warm it is, and they'll just stand still and let you do it, but sooner or later the air escapes again and the blemishes reappear over their eyes. There's only one way to be on guard against a trick like that: feel around the bones, make sure there are no air pockets there. And then there's the farce of them trying to sell somebody a blind horse! The officer waves a straw in front of its eyes to see if it gives any response, but what the horse is really responding to is the trader plunging his fist into its belly or its side, or, if he seems to be petting it nicely, it means he's got a nail hidden in the glove, so that he's actually pricking it when it looks like he's stroking it." I told the cavalry officer all this and ten times more, but it didn't get him anywhere: the next day I caught sight of him buying two pathetic heaps of horseflesh, one scragglier than the next, and he even called me over to come have a look and said to me, "Well now, brother, get a look here! I've got the hang of horse-buying pretty quick!"

I gave a quick glance, broke into a chortle, and replied that, well sir, there's nothing to see here. "This one's shoulders are too meaty, she'll be falling flat on her face all the time. This one rides too low – her hoof hits her belly, which'll be all ripped up inside of a year. And this one stomps her hoof while she's eating her oats and kicks against the wall of the paddock." I had put the kibosh on this sale, which, if you ask me, was all for the best.

The next day the prince said to me, "No, Ivan, I don't share your gift with horses. I think it's best if you come and work for me, as my connoisseur – you pick the horses, and I'll buy them."

I agreed at once and lived with him for three very happy years, not so much as a slave or hired hand but more as a friend and deputy, and probably could've saved up a pretty penny around then, if it hadn't all gone to drink, since how it usually works when a horse breeder comes to town is that he goes off with the army purchaser and sends someone he trusts to butter up the connoisseur. The breeders know it's not really the purchaser who calls the shots in these situations but the connoisseur. Like I told you, I'm a born connoisseur, and I took to my role with gusto, serving the man I knew I could never fully repay. My prince completely understood this and respected me all the more for it, and we lived together and got in the habit of being completely frank with each other. Some days, if he'd gambled away a lot the night before, he'd come out to the stables in the morning and find me, wearing his usual Asian tunic. He'd say, "Well now, my quasi-semi-respectable Ivan Severyanych! How are things with you?' He was always teasing me with nicknames like that, *quasi-semi-respectable* indeed! But his respect for me couldn't have been greater, as you'll see.

I knew very well what it meant when he talked to me like that, and so all I'd say in reply was, "Oh, just fine, sir. Things are going well, thanks be to God. And you, Your Grace, how are your circumstances?"

"Mine," he'd say, "have taken such a plunge that you shouldn't have bothered asking."

"Well, did Your Lordship blow some cash last night, as usual?"

"You guessed it, my kinda-sorta-upstanding companion. Lose, did I? Oh boy, did I ever."

"And how much has Your Grace been relieved of?"

He'd tell me how many thousands he'd lost, and I'd just shake my head and say, "What Your Excellency needs is a solid flogging – shame there's no one to give you one."

He'd burst out laughing and say, "That's just it, there isn't."

"Well sir, you go lay down on my cot and I'll lay some fresh matting under your head, and really lay into you."

He, of course, would start working on me, trying to get me to loan him the cash for another night at the tables. "No, better yet, forget my skin, give me a little of your expense money so I can try again – I can feel a victory coming on."

I'd answer, "Well, My Lord, I humbly thank you. But I've got to say no – try your luck all you want, but don't expect it to change."

"What do you mean, you thank me?" he'd say, lightly at first, but starting to get angry. "I say, please don't forget yourself with me. Stop acting as my custodian and give me the money right now."

We all asked Ivan Severyanych, had he given the prince the money for another try at his luck?

"Why, never!" he answered. "Either I'd make up a story about spending all the money to buy oats, or else I'd just bolt from the courtyard."

"But didn't that just make him madder?"

"Oh, it made him madder. He'd just come right out and say, 'Now, my halfway-partway-reasonable friend, you may consider yourself unemployed.'"

And I'd answer, "Well that works out just fine for me. Please give me back my passport."

"Alright," he'd say. "Get your things together, and your passport will be returned tomorrow."

But by the next day the entire flap would always be completely forgotten, and we never spoke of it ever again. It rarely took more than an hour before he'd come back in an awfully different frame of mind, and say, "Thank you, my astronomically irrelevant friend, for having the strength not to give me back the money I was asking for."

And that was how it always ended up. We became so close that if anything happened to me, even on my days off, he'd respond by rushing to my side like a brother."

"'Happened to you?' What happened to you?"

"I've already told you that I took days off sometimes."

"And what do you mean by 'days off'?"

"I'd leave the court and have some fun. Once I'd got a taste for wine, I drank it every single day, and never with moderation, but if something was really bothering me then I'd run off and drink as much as I could, hiding out for a couple days swilling like a fish. Sometimes it'd come over me with no warning at all. Like if we had to send the horses away for a while – and they're not exactly my kith and kin, are they? – but I'd get to missing them terribly and drink myself into a stupor. And especially if I had to be away from one of the handsomer beasts, I'd just miss him so much, the mongrel, and become really obsessed. I'd see him everywhere I looked, and there was only one escape."

"You mean drinking?"

"That's right – I'd go out and get smashed."

"Would you stay out long?"

"Well, that… depended. Some days I'd go out for a few drinks, and others I'd drink everything in sight and either get knocked around by someone or beat someone up myself. Other times it was shorter, and I'd pass the night in a police station or a ditch by the road, and wake up refreshed and head home. But I kept myself in line, and whenever I could feel it coming on I'd go to the prince and say, "Well, well, Your Excellency. Kindly relieve me of the money I have, I'm going to take off."

He had learned not to argue with me, but would just take the money, or sometimes ask, "Does Your Honor expect to be gone long?"

I would answer based on the strength of my wanderlust, and let him know whether to expect me back soon or not.

And then I'd go, leaving him to run the estate and wait for my return at the end of the time off, and it all went along without a hitch. But after a while I became disgusted with my own weakness, and decided then and there to cast it off forever. I took myself for one last day off, one so frightful it gives me the willies just to remember it."

XI

Naturally we pressed Ivan Severyanych to favor us even further with the story of this ill-fated time in his life, and he, good soul that he was, could not refuse. Here is what he told us about his "last day off":

We had a mare, a youthful, golden bay mare called Dido, bought from a stud farm and destined from her birth for an officer's saddle. She was a dream of a horse: the sweetest little head, handsome eyes, and wide nostrils that tapered out, so she never had trouble getting her breath. She had a light mane, a breast that sailed graciously from between her shoulders like a ship, her back sloped, pasterns banded white on feet so light that when she got them rolling it always looked like a game. To make a long story short, no sportsman could see the beauty of such an animal and ever forget it again. I took to her so strongly that I never wanted to leave the stables when she there, I'd just stand around and pet her for the sheer joy of it. Sometimes I'd stay there and scrub her down myself, head to toe, till there wasn't a fleck of dust anywhere on her, and I'd even plant little kisses on her forehead, right where that sweet golden curl came out. At that time two fairs were in town, one at L. and the other at K., so the prince and I split up to have them both covered. Suddenly I was brought a letter from him, that said to bring such and such horses – and Dido. I couldn't say what he needed my little beauty for, the apple of my huntsman's eye. But of course I figured someone must want to buy her, my little darling, or trade for her, or, worse yet, that he'd lost her at the card table. I sent Dido off with some stable boys, and then I became so bitterly lonesome that I decided to take a day off. Except I was in a funny spot. I've already told you about how I always did it – when the irresistible urge for a day off came over me, I'd hand the prince all my spending money, which tended to be an awful lot, and tell him, "Alright, I'm off for some-odd days, see you later." What was I supposed to do now, with the prince away from home? I thought to myself, "No, no, I mustn't drink a sip, without my prince here there's no one to hold onto the cash, yes yes all this cash, more than five thousand!" That was my decision, and I held to it firmly, much as I wanted to go out drinking. I expected the desire to subside, but it didn't – in fact it grew stronger and stronger, and then I thought, "Get a hold of yourself! There must be some way you can go out drinking *and* keep the prince's money safe!" I started hiding the money, hiding it in the most ingenious places where no one would ever look. I thought to myself, "What else can I do? It's obvious I can't master this desire. Better, yes better, that the money be tucked securely in here, where no one can get to it, and then I suppose I might as well go and have a day off after all." But as soon as I tried to leave I was assailed by a confusion: Where in blazes could I hide this damned money?! When I stepped out, I'd immediately envision somebody creeping over and stealing it. So I'd have to double back and grab it away and find another spot for it. I drove myself nuts shifting that money around – first in the haystacks, then in the cellar, next the eaves, and everyplace else I could think of, and just when I'd find a good spot, I'd be taken with the feeling that someone had seen me, so I'd grab it back and bury it, then dig it up and walk around with it a minute, and finally I thought to myself, "Enough already, it's just not happening, this is one wish I just can't give in to." And then I had a divine revelation: Who else could it be but Beelzebub himself that was torturing me like this, and what better tool to scare him off than the grace of the Almighty? I took myself to an early mass, said my prayers, secured my salvation, and then, while I was leaving the church, I saw that the wall was painted with an image of the Last Judgment, with angels accosting the Devil by swinging heavy chains at him. I fell into prayer right there, staring at the wall and entreating the help of the holy angels, and punched Satan right in his filthy mug while I shouted a little rhyme:

Well now, hey, here's a fig for you, aye
Whatever you want you can go out and buy!

Having said that I fell silent, and, having finally got my house in order, I headed to the tavern for a drink of tea.

When I got there, to the tavern I mean, milling around with all the other guests I saw an obvious scofflaw. Just the most low-down villainous knave. I'd seen this guy before and written him off as some mere charlatan or buffoon – he bounced around the fairs a lot, tugging at the gentlemen's sleeves to beg alms in French. He seemed to be from good people, maybe like he'd been in the service, even, but cards and drink had obviously ruined him and now he wandered across the world panhandling. Here he was, in the very tavern I'd wandered into, surrounded by a team of waiters who were trying to throw him out. He refused and stood there shouting, "Have you no sense! Do you know who I am?! Why, my station is far above yours. I used to own serfs just like you, and when I did I'd send them out to the barn to be whipped for nothing but my own amusement! I may have lost my fortune, but only because it was God's will, and I still bear the mark of his wrath. None of you would dare lay a finger on me!"

We all assumed it was just hot air and everyone started laughing at him, but he went on undeterred with stories of the grand life he'd lived, and the magnificent carriages he'd ridden round in, and how he'd expelled civilian gentlemen from the public gardens, and one time had even showed up naked at the house of the Governor's wife, "and now," he said, "now for its presumption my soul has been turned to stone, and vodka's the only way I can soften it – bring me some more! I've got no money to pay, but I'll eat the glass when I'm done!"

One of the guests ordered him one, to watch him

devour its receptacle after. He drank it down in one gulp and then just as he'd promised, everyone saw him bite into the glass and gobble it down, amusing and astonishing all of us. I was moved to pity – to think of it, a man of high birth so enslaved to the bottle that he'd trade his guts just for a drop! His bowels, I thought, could use a rinse after all that, so I ordered him another on my tab, one he wouldn't have to chew glass for. Asked him not to, in fact. This moved him deeply, and he came and offered me his hand.

"Surely," he said, "you were a man with a master, someone from the gentry?"

"That's so," I told him.

"I saw right away that you're not a swine like the other rabble in here," he said. "*Grand merci* for that."

"Forget about it. Go with God!"

"No, no," he answered, "I'm awfully glad to be talking with you. Slide over a minute, let me sit down."

"Sure, have a seat."

He plopped down next to me and started going on and on about what a great family he had come from and how top-notch his education had been. Then he said, "Wait a second – you're drinking tea?"

"Tea, sure. Have one with me."

"You're kind to offer," he said, "but it's not hot tea I love, it's frivoli-tea. Another glass of wine for me, maybe?" And he talked me into buying him a drink, then another, and a third, till it really started annoying me. But even more grating was the way he talked, all bluster and lies one minute and weepy self-effacements the next.

"Do you realize what kind of a man you're talking to? God created me the same year as the Emperor himself, and we're the same age."

"What of it?"

"Look what's become of me! Look at where I've ended up in spite of it all! I'm a complete nobody, practically a nonentity whom everyone despises!"

With these words he ordered another vodka, a whole carafe this time, and started intoning the whole never-ending story of how the merchants used to scoff at him when he went out to the taverns. Finally he said, "These uncultivated people, they think it's an easy burden to carry, roving around eternally and drinking and always eating the glass afterward. Well, let me tell you, it's not easy, brother, no it's a mighty heavy load! Most of them couldn't even pull it off, but I've had to train myself to do it, because, the way I see it, a man's got to bear his own burden whatever it is. That's what I'm doing."

"So tell me," I tried pressing him, "why this little habit of yours is so hard to kick. Why don't you just give it up?"

"Give it up? Oh no, brother, there's no way I could ever give it up"

"Why not?"

"Two reasons: first of all, when I haven't gotten a few drops I can never go to sleep, and I just wander the streets all night, and second, and even more important, my Christian sentiments don't allow it."

"How can that be? Don't get me wrong, it's easy to see how you'd never make it to bed, because you'd just be out all night wandering in search of booze. What I just can't believe is that your Christian sentiments would prevent you from putting an end to such filthy behavior!"

"Sure, you can't believe it. That's what they all say. But let's say I did dry out for a while; what then? Well sir, no sooner would I have dropped the habit than someone else would pick it up! And do you suppose that would be to his advantage?"

"Oh, Lord, no! No, I don't see how that could make anyone happy."

"Aha!" he shouted. "That's just it then. And since I'm fated to suffer like this, the least you could do is order me another carafe of vodka!"

I knocked the bar for another carafe, and stayed put because, to be honest, I'd begun to find him pretty amusing, and he went on with his sob story:

"It's not inappropriate that all this suffering should fall to me of all people, since I'm from a good family and have had a real education, so fine that even as a little boy I said my prayers in French. But I was ruthless and always caused people such misery, losing my serfs at cards, tearing mothers from their children, married myself off once to a rich lady and gave her such a hard time that she dropped dead. It was all my own fault, I knew perfectly well, but in my agony I even blamed God for making me such a shady character. That's why he punished me, changed my disposition so that I haven't got a trace of pride in anything; spit in my face and I'll just turn my cheek, long as there's some sauce on hand to help me forget myself."

"And you never mind this new disposition you've been given?"

"Mind it? No, I don't. You see, it may be worse, but it's better."

"Wait a second, wait a second. What do you mean, it's worse but it's better?"

"It's like this," he said. "Now at least I know that I'm the one destroying myself, and there's no one else I can destroy, since everyone's turned away from me. I," he went on, "am like Job in his sufferings, and here lies all my happiness and all my salvation." He gulped down his vodka and called for another carafe and said, "and just you remember, my dear friend, never pass judgment on another man – no one can know what hidden passions are the engine of his suffering. We, the accursed, we endure these sufferings for the common good. If you feel any affliction weighing down upon you, don't simply cast it off for another man to pick up, but instead seek one out who would willfully take on this weakness of yours."

"Where would you even find such a man? No one would agree to that!"

"How can you make such a pronouncement," he asked. "There are people who would agree to it, and you wouldn't have to look very far: one of them's sitting in front of you right now."

"Are you joking?"

Out of nowhere he leapt from his stool: "Joking? No, I'm not, and if you don't believe me, give it a go."

"How should I do that," I asked.

"That's very easy: you want to know how gifted I am? For you see, brother, I have a wonderful gift. Now, look here: I'm drunk. You tell me – am I drunk or am I not?"

I looked him over: he was turning slightly blue and wild-eyed and he couldn't stand up straight, and I said: "Yes, it would seem that you're quite drunk."

"Turn to the ikon in the corner for a minute, and say an 'Our Father' in your head."

I did as he said and turned toward the ikon, and had only just barely made it through "Our Father" before that debauched little baronet was bossing me around again: "Now, come back and have another look at me – am I drunk now, or not?"

I turned around and saw he was sober as a judge, standing there, smiling. "How can this be – what's your secret?" I asked.

And he answered, "It's no secret at all, but what they call *magnetism*."

"I don't understand. What's that?"

"It's a kind of radiance that can be put into a man, and then nothing can chase it out of him, not sleep or booze or anything. It's a gift. I'm making this demonstration to you so you'll know that I could quit drinking any time I want, cold turkey, and never touch the stuff again. It's just that I don't want someone else picking up the habit, or to find myself straying from the straight and narrow path I'm finally walking. But I'm always ready to help someone else give up the bottle forever."

"By all means then!" I shouted. "Please, do it for me!"

"Would you say you are a drinker?"

"Oh, I would say so indeed, sir, and sometimes to a most extreme degree."

"Don't you worry, friend. I can heal you with my own two hands. It'll allow me to thank you for all your hospitality tonight!"

"Please, do me the favor, take it from me!"

"Very well, my friend, very well. I'll take this burden from you completely, and, to show my gratitude, I'll take it all upon myself." and he called out for a bottle of wine and two glasses.

"What are the wineglasses for?"

"One is for me, and one is for you."

"Yes, but I won't be drinking."

"Oh tsk! *Silence!* Be quiet! Who are you, the doctor or the patient?!"

"Okay, okay, have it your way. I'll be the patient."

"Which makes me the doctor. I'll make the diagnoses and hand out the medicines, thank you." With that, he poured us each a glass and started whirling his hands around above mine like a precentor. He whirled and whirled and barked out an order: "Drink!"

I wasn't without misgivings, but, to be totally honest, a couple sips of wine sounded pretty good, and he really wanted me to drink and kept shouting, and finally I thought, "Maybe I'd better have a few swigs, just to see what happens!" I emptied my glass.

"How's it taste – good, or soured?"

"I don't know, it's… hard to say."

"All that means is you haven't had enough yet," he said, and he poured me another glass and again started waving his arms around over it. He waved and waved and ended it in a sudden *bop*, and again had me gulp the whole thing down. "Well, how was that one?"

I felt like yanking his a chain a little, so I said, "This one was a little rough, actually."

He poured me a third, with all the same wild gesticulations, and again he commanded me "Drink!" and I did, and I said, "Ah, now that one went down easier," and then I reached over for the carafe and poured us both some more, and we kept right on drinking. He still wouldn't let me sip from anything his hands hadn't whirled around over, and he'd even grab my hands and push them away and say, "Shoo! *Silence, attendez*!" and then he'd wave his hands over it and say, "Now it's ready, and thou shalt receive, as it is written!"

I received my treatment from this fallen noble with whom I lingered in the tavern till evening, and I felt greatly at peace, since I knew I was drinking not as an indulgence but as a privation. I felt inside my coat for the money. All still there where it belonged, I returned to my drinking.

The Baron, having got drunk with me, proceeded to tell me everything, how he'd squandered his life carousing and malingering, and after everything else, that's what got us fighting, that he accused me of knowing nothing about love.

"So what if I don't? How's that my fault? You should just be glad that you do know all about it, and have bloomed into such a splendid specimen because of it."

And he replied, "Sh, *silence*! Love is a sanctuary!"

"Nonsense, my friend."

"Buddy, you're a scoundrel if you'd really scoff at the heart's most sacred emotion and call it nonsense!"

"Well, but nonsense is what it is."

"Do the words 'Beauty is nature's perfection' mean nothing to you?"

"All that means anything to me is the beauty of a horse."

He leapt to his feet and tried to box my ears.

"You seriously think a horse represents beauty, the perfection of nature?"

But he never got the chance to press his point, since it was already quite late and the bartender, seeing how drunk we'd got, had winked at the bouncers, six of them, who came over to us and said, "Time to leave," as they scooped us up in their giant arms and tossed us out on the street. Then they slammed the door behind them and locked it.

And that was when it began, a phantasmagoria that, no matter how many years go by, I can never understand or even remember in any great detail, leaving me with almost no idea what happened to me, or what power it operated by, but knowing only that I was prey to such temptations and misadventures as you never read about in the Book of Saints.

XII

First thing I thought to do as I was sailing down to the street was reach in my pocket and feel for my wallet. Still there – good. "Now," I thought, "just make sure you get it home safely."

A dark night, the darkest you can imagine. Back home around Kursk we get nights like that in summer, pitch-dark but sweltering, tranquil, stars dangling from the sky like ikon-lamps, a darkness so thick that you can feel it against your skin, feeling you back. With the fair in town, the streets would be swarming with people, the kind of people who'd rob or kill you as soon as shake your hand. Even though I can handle myself in a fight, a few things were worrying me: first of all, I was drunk; second, they could come up in a gang, ten or more guys maybe, and I doubted I'd have the strength to fight off a whole crowd myself; and third, I remembered how back at the bar, every time I'd had to get off my stool to settle up, my drinking buddy, the fallen little Baron, could see the fat wad of banknotes bulging from my tunic. And that's when I started to wonder whether this guy had something up his sleeve. Come to think of it, where was he? Hadn't we been tossed out together? Where could he possibly have scooted off to so fast?

I stood up and stealthily glanced around me. Not knowing what name to call him, I started cooing out, "Hey, you there? Hey, magnet man, where are you?"

Suddenly, he rose up before my eyes like some vile apparition and said, "Here I am."

His voice seemed suddenly unfamiliar, and there in the darkness even his features were somehow changed.

"Come on over," I said. "Little closer, little closer." As he approached I grabbed him by the shoulder blades and started to look him over real close. I didn't recognize this person at all – who was he? For some reason, just as soon as I touched him, my memory got completely scrambled and I couldn't tell what anything was. All I heard was him muttering in French: *dee-kah-tee-lee-kah-tee-pay* – I couldn't catch a word.

"What in blazes are you mumbling?"

"Dee-kah-tee-lee-kah-tee-pay."

"Come on already, you numbskull! Tell me who you are, tell me in simple Russian, and tell me right now! I can't for the life of me remember you."

"Dee-kah-tee-lee-kah-tee-pay. It is I, the magnetizer!"

"Oh to hell with you, you wretched urchin!" And suddenly my memory came flooding back, but when I leaned in for a closer look, I saw that he had two noses! Two noses, what do you know! As soon as I started trying to wrap my mind around the implications of that – I completely forgot who he was again.

"Damn you," I thought. "How could I have ended up with a good-for-nothing like you?" I asked him again who he was, and again all he said was, "I'm the magnetizer."

"You keep your distance! How do I know you're not the Devil?"

"I'm not," he replied, "but you're not too far off." I clocked him in the forehead, and he got upset. "What are you hitting me for? I perform this great service for you, curing your alcoholism just like that, and you thank me with your fists?"

No matter how hard I tried, I couldn't remember who he was. "Tell me who you are already!" He answered, "Me? I'm your lifelong friend."

"Alright, stranger, if we're such good friends, does that mean you'd never do me any harm?"

"Nope," he said, "but I'll give you such a *petit-comme-peut* you'll feel like a whole new man."

"Come on," I answered. "I know when I'm being lied to."

"Honest to God," he said, "honest to God – oh what a *petit-comme-peut*!"

"What a load of hot air! Stop talking French you filthy animal – I have no idea what a *petit-comme-peut* is!"

"I'm going to give you a whole new perspective."

"Oh, really? What kind of a perspective would that be?"

"A perspective from which you can understand that beauty is nature's perfection!"

"And just how," I pressed on, "is that understanding going to suddenly appear in my brain?"

"Come along and I'll show you."

"Alright then, let's go."

So we went. The two of us could barely walk, yet walk we did. I had no idea where we were headed, but periodically I'd stop and suddenly remember that I had no idea who I was walking with, and I'd say again, "Stop! Tell me, who are you? Tell me or I'm stopping right here."

He'd tell me, but I'd only remember for a minute, and again I'd have to ask, "How come I can't seem to remember who you are?"

He answered, "That's just an effect of my magnetism, but don't be afraid, it'll wear off soon. Let me give you more magnetism, a bigger dose this time."

Suddenly he whipped around behind my back, and started twiddling around with my hair… it felt miraculous, like he was getting ready to climb inside my head.

"Listen here, you! Who the devil are you? What are you rummaging around for back there?"

"Easy, easy," he replied, "and for goodness' sake stand still! I'm introducing the full spectrum of my magnetism into you."

"Yes, yes, the full spectrum, sure. Are you sure you're not planning to rob me, though?"

He said no.

"Hang on a second, friend, I'll be the judge of that." I reached in to feel for the money again – still safe.

"Well now, alright, alright, you're no thief," but as for

who he was, I'd forgotten again. I'd even forgotten how to ask, but it was just as well, because now I'd become preoccupied with this completely strange feeling that he'd climbed right inside me through the base of my head and was seeing the world through my eyes, yes, the portholes of my eyes.

I couldn't believe what a fast one he'd pulled. "Would you please explain," I said, "what you've done to my eyesight?"

"Eyesight?" he said. "Ah, it's gone now."

"What are you talking about?! What do you mean, it's gone?"

"What I mean," he answered calmly, "is that if you look now, all you can see is what isn't there."

"Quit talking in riddles! Alright, let's see what you're on about."

So I opened my eyes and stared as deep as I could into the darkness. What did I see but faces, horrible wrenched faces peering back at me from every corner, dancing around on their vile little legs, darting out across the path in front of me, lingering at the streetcorners, biding their time and chanting, "Let's kill him, yes, and take all his treasure!" And there in front of me again was my scraggly little Baron, his whole face illuminated, and behind me I heard some bedlamite clamor of voices and twanging instruments, all manner of squeak and squawk, hysterical cackling. I looked around again and saw that I was standing with my back to some kind of a house, light pouring from its open windows, and all the voices and clatter and whining guitar were coming from inside it, and there in front of me again was the

Baron, waving his hands in front of my face and stopping over my chest, pressing down on my heart, then grabbing my fingers and yanking them around a minute, and he was going at it with such vigor that you could see he was bathed in sweat.

Just then, standing in front of that house with the light streaming from its windows, I began to snap out of it, came back to my senses. Suddenly I wasn't afraid of him anymore.

"Listen to me, whoever you are, Devil himself or just some vexing demon, wicked ghoul, whatever, just do me a favor: either wake me up or begone from my sight!"

"Wait, you're not ready yet. There's still the danger that you won't be able to take it."

"What is it," I asked, "that I won't be able to take?"

"What's happening in the celestial spheres."

"What do you mean? I don't hear anything too special going on."

He insisted that I hadn't been paying attention, so he told me in the language of God, "If thou wouldst hear, make ye as he who playeth the psaltery, he who inclineth his head to the heavens, who lendeth his ear to the Lord's song, who striketh the string with his hand."

"Well now," I thought, "what's all this? He doesn't sound so drunk, suddenly. No, he's not talking like a drunk now at all!"

He kept staring me down, and quietly flailing around in front of me, and kept trying to get me to do his bidding.

"Hearken thou unto the strings," he went on, "and see with what brilliancy one hand striketh them and then another, and how the harp bringeth a song unto the Lord, and how the player himself rejoiceth in the sweet honey of the tune!"

I tell you, it was just as though I had heard not words, but the waters of life themselves coursing past my ear, and I thought to myself, "Some drunk you turned out to be! Listen to him, he speaks the Word of God!"

And just like that, the Baron stopped flailing and said, "Well now, that's enough of that! Now wake up – wake up and be strengthened!"

With that, he leaned down and started fishing around in his pocket for something, and, finally, emerged with it. It looked like an itty-bitty cube of sugar, all covered in lint and filth from being in there too long. He picked off the dirt with his nails, blew it clean, and said, "Open up!"

"What for?" I asked, and opened my mouth wide. He deposited the lump of sugar on my lip.

"Suck," he said, "and suck with courage! This is a magnetic sugar-mentor and it will make you strong."

Even though he was speaking French, I realized he was talking about magnetism. So I didn't ask any more questions, just kept busy sucking that sugar cube, and besides, suddenly I realized he was nowhere to be found.

Where he'd stolen off to in the darkness or what he did there the Lord only knows: all I knew was that I was standing there alone and back to my old self again. I thought, "What am I waiting for? It's time to go home." But I still had a problem: I didn't know what street I was on or whose house I was loitering in front of. I thought, *Is there really*

a house there at all? Maybe it's just an apparition, a... hal-
lucination. But it's nighttime, everyone's asleep – so why are the
lights on? Well, old man, I guess I should go have a look... I'll
creep up and have a look: if there's actual people inside, I'll ask
them what street we're on so I can get home. And if instead of
real live people I see nothing but seductive phantasms – well,
what's the worst that could happen? I'll just intone the words,
"This ground is holy: get thee behind me!" and everything will
vanish.

XIII

Having made up my mind, I ambled over to the porch, crossed myself, made obeisances to God and – nothing. Nothing! The house just stood there, it didn't even wobble, and I could see that through the open doors, down at the end of a long hall, there were sconces that held lit candles, each dangling from a nail driven into the wall. When I peered in more closely, I could see that to the left there were more matted doors, which had these very strange little candelabra dangling over them, ornamented with stars cut out of mirror. I think to myself, "What kind of a house can this be? It doesn't seem to be an inn, and yet it does seem open to the public, but just what could be going on in there I can't even guess." I froze up, kept my ears open, and as I listened I could hear the strains of a song pouring through the matted doors... Oh, that melody that seemed to faint, just heart-wrenching, and singing it, oh what a voice! A bell that rang crimson, a song that just stole your heart and held it so you'd never get it back. I stood there, transfixed, and then I saw a door opening up across the long hall, and through it waltz these two gypsies, a tall one in silk breeches and a velvet Cossack's coat showing another one through a private doorway that I hadn't noticed before under the sconces. Though I confess I didn't get a good luck at him, I'm pretty sure it was no gypsy at all, but my magnetizer! I could hear the gypsy saying, "Alright, alright my darling, don't be mad about the half-ruble. Come back tomorrow: if we find some use for him, you'll get a finder's fee."

At that, he bolted the door behind him and ran over, pretending he'd just noticed me. He opened one of the matted doors and said, "I beg your pardon, gentleman merchant. Please, come into our house, and hear our beautiful songs! Oh, what voices you'll hear." With that, he stopped talking and swung the door open in front of me.

My dear gentlemen, I couldn't tell you just what came over me then, but I was suddenly overcome by the most profound feeling that I'd been there before, almost like I'd come home. The room was, well, it was huge, with a low ceiling that hung even lower toward the middle, like its belly was bulging out, and the air so clouded with smoke that you could barely make out the chandelier. Underneath the smoke the haze of people was almost as thick... so many of them – more than I could count, gathered together in front of the source of that voice I'd heard – a young gypsy girl. The song was just winding down as I came in, last note lingering tenderly, and tenderly dying off into the smoke... that voice, that sweet and wonderful voice, it just died there, and the crowd drifted into a rapture so silent that they seemed to have died with it. But after a minute of that they broke into wild hoots of appreciation, slapping palms and hemming and hawing. I was thunderstruck: Who were all these people, these innumerable faces that appeared in greater and greater numbers the deeper I looked into the smoke? "Gracious!" I thought. "Can they really be people? Demons have the power to take human shape…" But then I spotted several gentlemen of the cavalry whom I knew, and some horse breeders, too, and some fancy merchants and landowners I'd come across because they had a thing for horses, and in the midst of all of them was this gypsy girl, a girl like… I can't even call her a woman, she was like some brightly colored snake swaying on her tail, her long body writhing, a fire raging in her wild black eyes. What a vision! She was carrying a tray lined with flutes of champagne encircling a little heap of money. Silver was all it lacked: no room for silver with all that gold and all those banknotes, five ruble blue titmice, ten ruble red grouses, twenty-five ruble gray ducks, – aha, but no white swans! They weren't throwing hundreds at her. I saw how it worked: she offered you a drink, and you took it and threw back as much cash as you felt like, gold or banknotes, and then she leaned over and kissed you on the lips, and then parted with a curtsy. She went up the first row, down the second – the guests were arranged in a kind of a semi-circle – and when she came to the very last row, which I was standing behind, she finished and turned back, giving me the cold shoulder, but then an old gypsy shouted out, "Grusha!" and pointed me out with his eyes. She flitted her lashes at him – oh, oh my God, what lashes they were, so long and full, black, alive on their own, flitting around like birds, and after he'd yelled at her, her eyes exploded into a fury and shot fire at him. Even so, she followed his infuriating command, doing as she was told, came up to me in the back room, curtsied, and said, "Dear sir, won't you have a drink to my health?"

I couldn't even muster an answer, she had so enchanted me! Especially when she bowed her head over the tray and I could suddenly see how from the thick black hair at the part a streak ran down her back like a thread of silver and disappeared, I went completely mad! That's the only way to say it. I drank it right down, and held up the glass for a while to study her face through it. I couldn't tell whether she was light-skinned or dark, but you could see an incredible vibrancy just under her skin, like a plum in streaming sunlight, and there was a vein beating in her temple. "Well now," I thought, "now *here* we see a case where beauty really *is* the perfection of nature. The magnetizer spoke true: it's nothing like the beauty of a horse, a mere beast offered for sale."

I drank the whole glass down to the bottom and slammed it back onto the tray, and she just stood there, waiting to see what price I'd offer for the pleasures of her touch. I plunged my hand into my pocket to find something to give her, but all I had was some change, twenty-kopeck and quarter-ruble coins – *not enough*, I thought, *for such a charming little snake, and besides I don't want to look like some kind of ne'er-do-well*. I could even hear the gentlemen muttering to the gypsy, and not even very quietly, "Oh, Vasiliy Ivanov, how can you send Grusha to treat a bum like that? It offends us, frankly."

"Gentlemen, gentlemen," he said, "my daughter is only performing the custom of our gypsy ancestors! We treat all our guests the same, with dignity and respect. Please, do not take offense. Don't you know, even the simplest man can appreciate talent and true beauty. Indeed, it's rather a common occurrence."

I couldn't help overhearing the whole thing, and I thought, "Ach, the wolves take you all! You think if you're richer than me that makes your feelings richer too? I should say not! No, what has to be will be – I can repay the prince later, for now I won't stand to be disgraced or to belittle this matchless beauty!"

With this thought, I reached into my shirt, pulled out a roll of hundred-ruble swans, and slapped it onto the tray. The little gypsy girl balanced the tray on one hand, and with the other she pulled out a white handkerchief and touched it to my lips, and she, well, didn't kiss me so much as just brush her lips against mine, and it was as though she left them with a light, poisonous residue before she turned and walked away.

I stayed in one place while she left, and then that one old gypsy, Grusha's father, grabbed me by one arm while some other gypsy took me by the other, and they dragged me forward and deposited me in a chair in the front row next to the local police chief and a few other gentlemen.

I wasn't too keen on this, frankly – I'd had enough and felt ready to leave. They kept me there, though, calling her over again, "Oh, Grusha, little Grunyushka, keep our valued guest entertained!"

She drew close again, and the devil only knows what witchcraft she could work with those eyes, but one glance and that was it, I'd caught the bug. "Please, do not insult us: visit here at our house a while longer."

"How could anyone be willing to offend *you*," I said, and sat back down.

She kissed me again, and again there was that strange sensation, as if she'd brushed me with some mysterious poison that set all the blood in my body boiling madly up to my heart, burning with eagerness.

It all started up again, the singing and merriment, a different gypsy girl this time making rounds with the champagne. Don't get me wrong, this one was a real cutie too, but next to my Grusha? No, she didn't have half Grusha's loveliness, and so all I threw her was a couple of silver quarter-rubles. The gentlemen got a good laugh out of it, but I didn't care – I could still see where she was standing, my little Grushenka, and I was biding time till she had another solo. But she didn't have another. She just sat around with the others, singing in the chorus, and all I could look at were her lips and her little white teeth… "Oh," I thought, "oh, my sweet little orphan. Only a minute has passed, and I've lost a hundred rubles, and now I'll never hear her sing again!" But to my relief I wasn't the only one longing to hear more of her, and all the gentlemen of note and other valued guests shouted out one after another: "Grusha! Grusha! Grusha! Grusha! Grusha! 'The Skiff!'"

And what do you know, the gypsies all cleared their throats, her little brother gave his guitar a strum, and she started singing. Their singing is always so moving, and it just melts your heart, and she had that voice, the same one I'd just barely heard echoing down the hall, how it moved me! I can't tell you how deeply. She started out guttural, almost masculine: "The seee-eee-eeea is thraaa-aaa-aaashing, the seee-eee-eeeaaaa is craa-aaaaa-aaashing." She had such passion that you could just hear the little skiff churning about on perilous waves. Then suddenly her voice changed, as the song addressed itself to the stars:

Oh, sweetest golden star
That welcomes in the morning,
All my sorrows seem afar
With you above me soaring

Then, just like that, another change. All their songs have these entreaties in them: they weep, they writhe, they tear your soul from your body, and then, suddenly, it's as though none of that had happened, and gladness wells up in your heart. That's just how it happened here to the little 'skiff' on the 'sea': the entire choir suddenly burst out in unison:

Ja–la–la., ja–la–la!
Ja–la–la pringala!

Ja-la-la pringa-la!
Hai da chepuringalya!
Hey hup-hai, ta gara!
Hey hop-hai-ta gara!

Afterward, little Grusha again brought around a tray of wine, and I pulled out another swan from under my coat… they shot me cold stares, as if my extravagance masked a desperation. But I didn't care in the least; I burned to bear my heart, to offer up my soul! I gave her a swan for every song she sang till I lost count, so that whenever anyone else asked her to sing she'd demure with a quick, "but I'm tired," while all I had to do was wink at the old gypsy, to say, *well my friend, can't you get her to give me a song?*, and he'd wave her over to me with his eyes and she'd get right back to serenading me. Song after song she sang, one more enchanting than the last, and I rewarded her so handsomely, swans beyond number, until at last, I have no idea how late but the sunlight was beginning to show through, she was completely sung out and exhausted, and shooting me a pointed look she went into one that began, "Fare you well, don't look back, begone from mine eyes." The lyrics seemed to be urging me along, but then the next line begged me to stay: "Or would you stay, my wild heart to amuse, while all the while my beauty's strength does you abuse?" That called for another swan! She gave me another kiss, so forceful it was nearly a bite, the dark flame roaring in her eyes, while the other gypsies marked the evil hour with a refrain of farewell:

Oh my sweet, but you must know
Of how, my dear, I love you love, so!

All the gypsies joined in and looked at Grusha, so I looked at her too, crooning, "you must know!" And then all the gypsies started singing, "Move along, little cottage, move along, little bed; the master needs someplace to lay his old head!" – and suddenly they all leapt up to dance. Gypsies dancing, dancing gypsies, so many of them wiggling around together that it seemed the cottage itself would start rolling. The gypsy girls pranced from gentleman to gentleman, getting their attention and then running away to be chased, by the young men with a catcall, the old ones with a groan. In a minute, I was the only one left in the room. Even the older men of distinction, who you'd think would have aged out past that kind of buffoonery, had all gallivanted off. At first they'd tried keeping glued to their seats, the more respectable ones, and, used as they were to avoiding shameful public shenanigans, they'd just sit there, eyeing the whole crazy business and tugging at their whiskers. Then one of these little minxes would come up and pull on one's shoulder, or else tug at his leg, and he'd jump right out of his seat and even he didn't know the moves he'd be doing on the dance floor, throwing himself around, acting the fool. The roly-poly little police chief jumped in with his two sons-in-law and started flapping around like a catfish, clunking around in his heavy boots, while a mounted hussar officer, a captain in rank and a wealthy young man, plus a suave dancer to boot, put everyone else to shame – hands at his hips, his heels flying and then crashing back onto the floor, showboating for all to see. He'd wiggle over toward one of the girls and open his arms like he was about to embrace her, and whenever he got close to Grusha he'd toss his head back and fling his hat at her feet, calling out, "Step on it, my beloved, my paramour!" And she, oh! What a dancer she was! I'd seen dancing girls in the theater before, but believe me, compared to my Grushenka they were just so many cavalry horses parading around lifelessly for show, just up to regulations, none of the spark of life flashing within them. But oh, how this lovely went sailing, like the barque of a Pharaoh! Her body twisting this way and that, supple as a snake, and you could almost hear the marrow inside her pouring itself from bone into bone, accommodating those marvelous twists and turns, and when she stopped it was with her back curled elegantly and her eyebrow right in line with her foot. What a work of art! Just looking at her was enough for the lot of us to lose our minds, burning with no thoughts, no memories, some with tears in our eyes, some showing our teeth, and everyone hollering, "Take all we have, just dance for us!" and, senselessly, they kept heaping money at her feet, some gold, some banknotes. The crowd of dancers got thicker and thicker, me sitting alone to the side, not knowing how many more times I could bear to see her stomp that damned hussar's cap. Every time, I could feel the blood becoming silk in my veins, the devil's work, and again she'd stomp it, and again, till finally I thought, "What do I need to torture myself for? Doesn't my heart deserve to come out of its cage to play?" and so I rose to my feet and shoved the hussar out of my way so I could start cutting a rug for Grusha. To help her finally forget all about that hussar and his hat, well, I hatched a little idea: "All of you," I thought, "can prattle on about how you'll give away all you have, but money talks. I'll show you how it looks when a man *really* cuts loose!" I reached in to grab a swan and shoved it under her foot, shouting, "Trounce it! Give it a good stomp!" At first, you could see she didn't know what to do – my swan was worth more than that hussar's cap, but she just ignored it, fixing her attention on the blasted hussar. But then, finally, the old gypsy, oh thank you! He saw what was going on and stomped his own foot at her. She got the message and sidled over to me… but she was furious and staring ferociously at the ground like a dragon in a fairy story getting ready to torch it, and I was twirling like a mad demon in front of her, and every time I took a leap I'd toss her another swan… I had her on such a pedestal that it verged on worship, and I caught myself thinking, "Well, is it you, accursed beauty, who created the heavens and the earth?" and I didn't shy away from screaming "Faster now, go faster!" swans upon swans under her feet, until, on one journey my arm made to reach for some, it felt only a dozen or so left. "The hell with you," I thought, "and the devil take the whole lot of you!" as I crumpled the rest of them into a little heap and threw it at her feet, then grabbed a bottle of Champagne from the table, smashed it at the neck, and shrieked, "Make room, my soul, or be drowned!" as I gulped down the entire bottle in one enormous swig to her health, since all that twirling around had left me desperate for a drink.

XIV

"What happened next?" we breathlessly asked Ivan Severyanych.

"Actually, it all unfolded just as he said it would."

"Who said it would?"

"Why, the magnetizer, the one who cast that spell on me. He'd promised he'd cure me of the devil of drink, and sure enough I haven't drunk a sip from that day on. Oh, he cured me all right."

"How did you ever deal with the prince over the swans you set free?"

"That was no big deal. Actually I can hardly believe how simple it was. I couldn't tell you myself how I made it home from that gypsy house, and I still don't remember going to sleep that night. The next thing I knew I could hear the prince rapping at my door and calling after me. I wanted to climb down from the chest I slept on, but I couldn't find the edge of it. I crawled over to one end of it, no edge there, so then I crawled across to the other – none there either! Totally turned around up there, and that's all there was to it! The prince bellowed out, "Ivan Severyanych!" All I could say back was, "One minute!" while I crawled around in all directions, until finally I thought, "Well, if you can't climb down, jump off," so I leapt as far forward as I could, and the next thing I knew I was feeling something smash into my face while everything around me starting ringing and clanging, everywhere including behind me, and I heard the prince's voice commanding his orderly, "Grab a candle – hurry!"

I stood perfectly still – I couldn't tell whether or not I was dreaming, yes dreaming, maybe, having still not found the edge of the chest, but when the orderly arrived with the candle I saw that I was standing up on the floor, had smashed my face through the glass door of a cabinet and shattered all the crystal in it.

"How could you have gotten so disoriented?"

"Easily. When I stumbled home from the gypsies' place I must've thought I was lying down on my chest like I do every night, only this time it was actually the floor. That's why I couldn't find the edges, and so of course when I jumped... I was wandering around because he – that, that *magnetizer* – when he drove the drinking devil out of me, he put the wandering one in instead! Suddenly what he'd said came back to me: "Of course, quitting drink *could* make everything worse..." I went off looking for him, so I could ask him to demagnetize me back to the way I was, only I never found him. It seemed that he'd taken so much onto himself that in the end he couldn't bear up, and he'd gone to an inn across the way from the gypsy place and drank himself to death."

"So you stayed magnetized?"

"I certainly did."

"And did this magnetism stay with you a long time?"

"Long time? For all I know I'm *still* magnetized."

"Be that as it may, I'd love to know what finally happened between you and that prince? I can't imagine how you explained to him that none of his swans were still around!"

"I explained it, but it turned out to be of no consequence. You see, the prince had lost all his money just like I had, only he lost his at the card table. So he came to ask for some money, and I just said, "Leave it alone already! Besides, I have no money."

He thought I must be joking. I tried to set him straight. "No sir, it's the God's honest. While you were gone I had a pretty big day off."

"How could you possibly have spent five thousand in a single day off?!"

"I threw it all at a gypsy girl."

He didn't believe me. I went on. "Well, take it or leave it, I'm telling you the truth."

That was that! He flew into a rage: "Shut the door, I'll show you how to waste government money!" But a minute later he changed his mind suddenly. "Alright, never mind. I'm just as reckless as you are." He went back to his room to lie down, and I headed to the hayloft to catch some sleep myself. When I came to, I was in the hospital. They informed me that I'd gone over into a delirium tremens and tried to hang myself, but, thank God, they put me in a straitjacket before I could do myself any serious harm. Later, when I was better, I went to see the prince on his estate, since by then he'd resigned his commission. I said, "Your Excellency, on my honor I must serve you to repay my debt."

"Oh, go to hell, you."

I could see he was completely ticked off, so I walked over to him and bowed my head.

"What the hell is that supposed to mean?" he asked.

"At least give me as bad a beating as I deserve!"

"Why are you talking to me as though I were cross, when for all you know I might not think any of this is your fault!"

"You can't be serious. Not my fault? How can it not be my fault that I went and just threw away that truckload of money? Believe me, sir, I know it all too well: the gallows is too good for a scamp like me."

"What else could you do, brother? You're an artist."

"What? How do you mean?"

"Here's how, Ivan Severyanych, you old so-and-so. I mean that you, my sorta-somewhat-respectable little friend, are an artist."

"I don't follow you."

"Don't take it the wrong way. You see, I myself am an artist."

"Well," I thought, "one thing's for sure – I'm not the only one who's got the deetees."

He got up, knocked his pipe into the ground, and said,

"It's no great mystery to me why you threw at her all the money you had – you see, brother, I myself gave her everything, more than I have, more than I have ever had."

My eyes were glued to him. "Oh, boss, my old friend, I mean, Your Excellency, have pity. It's scary to hear you talk this way."

"You have no reason to be frightened: God is infinite in his mercy, and maybe there'll be some way out. But as it stands, I've given over fifty thousand to the gypsy camp for Grusha."

I let out a gasp. "Fifty thousand?! For that little gypsy? You really think the little snake is worth it?"

"Now listen to you, my little halfway-somewhat-decent buddy, listen to you running your mouth like an idiot. An artist would never say that. What is she worth?! A woman is worth everything in the world, for she can cast a hex over you that you can't cure with a whole kingdom to throw at it, but she herself can take it from you any time she wants, just like that."

I had to agree that what he said made sense. Still, I couldn't help shaking my head, saying, "Oh, but such a price! A full fifty thousand!"

"I know," he said, "and please stop reminding me. I'm lucky they accepted that much. There's no amount I wouldn't have paid."

"You should've spat right in their faces! That would've been that."

"I couldn't do that, brother. I couldn't spit at them."

"Why not?"

"Because she'd stung with me her beauty and her gift for song, and I needed to heal or I'd go out of my mind. Admit it, though, she's something. Am I right? I mean, has she or hasn't she got a quality that just drives you mad with desire?"

I bit my lip, nodding my head wordlessly as if to say, "Oh, it's the truth alright."

"For me," the prince went on, "it's nothing to die for a woman. Can you understand that, how it is to be ready to die for love?"

"There's nothing hard to understand about it: beauty is nature's perfection."

"And just what exactly do you mean by that?"

"I mean," I replied, "that beauty is nature's perfection, and for a man who falls under its spell, even to die might be… a joy!"

"Well said, sir!" replied my prince. "Oh, very well said, my almost-halfway-nearly-respectable, my mini-micro-brained Ivan Severyanych! That's exactly right – to die would be a joy, and that's why it feels so sweet turning my life around for her. I've already quit my position, mortgaged my estate, and from now on I'll just live here, never seeing a soul, all the time looking only upon her face."

At this I quieted my voice to a whisper: "How can you look on her face here? Is she somewhere around?"

"Where else would she be? Of course she's here."

"How can that be?"

"Just wait here a second and you can see for yourself. I'll bring her right over – you're an artist, Ivan Severyanych, I don't have the heart to keep you from seeing her."

With this he headed out, leaving me alone. While I stood there, waiting, I thought, "Oh, this is no good at all, this rule that you'll look at no one's face but hers. You'll get bored!" But I didn't consider the specific implications much further, because suddenly I remembered that she was coming, and at once I got hot all over and my thoughts started swimming. *Am I really going to see her again?* And then, just like that, in they walked: the prince in front, a guitar with a big scarlet strap in one hand, and my Grushenka in the other, his one hand clasping both of hers, dragging her behind him like a conquest, resisting, looking away. Those black eyelashes with their quiver like the stir of a bird's wing.

The prince led her in, scooped her into his arms, and set her down like a child on the wide, soft divan with her feet in the corner. Then he slipped a velvet cushion under her back and another one under her arm, and laid the guitar strap across her shoulders and pulled her fingers up to the strings. He sat himself on the floor next to the divan and rested his head against the scarlet morocco of her slipper, and nodded at me as though to say *Now you sit down too*.

So I did, without saying a word: sat myself down cross-legged and stared at her. The room fell ghostly silent. I sat and sat, sat until my kneecaps ached, but any time I looked over at her she'd just be sitting exactly the same way, and if I looked at the prince I could see that he'd nearly gnawed off his mustachio from the darkness he felt – still, he hadn't said a word.

I nodded at him, as if to say, *Well, what are you waiting for? Get her to sing!* He answered in a sort of pantomime that he didn't know how.

There we were, both of us just sitting on the floor waiting for something to happen, when out of nowhere her motionless silence burst into a fit of heaving breaths and pitiful sobs, tears tracing her eyelashes, her fingers swarming across the guitar strings like wasps, and she started to hum. And then, oh so very quietly, in a voice that sounded almost like she was weeping, she sang out. "Oh good people, listen to my sorrow, the aching of my heart…"

"You see?" the prince whispered.

I whispered my reply to him in French: "*Petit-comme-peut*," I said, and that's as far as I got because suddenly she cried out, "And for my beauty they'll sell me away," and flung the guitar into the middle of the room, tore the scarf from her head, which she thrust — bawling now — into the cushions of the sofa. When I saw all this I also began to cry, and the prince broke down crying too, and grabbed the guitar and began, well, not exactly singing so much chanting, as though he was leading a church service, "Grant me rest, oh restless one, be my luck, oh luckless one." I saw her begin to take notice of how cruelly he was suffering, the tears he was crying and his song, and she began to calm herself down, compose herself, and suddenly she was wrapping her arms around his face, tenderly as a mother.

I could see she was feeling pretty sorry for him, and that

she'd comfort him, ease the pain of his heart in its longing. I stood up, ever so quietly, and crept away unnoticed.

"It must be then that you entered the monastery?" someone asked the storyteller.

"No, it wasn't then, it was a long time after," Ivan Severyanych answered, adding that much still lay in store for him to do with that woman, with whom his fate was entwined, that he would be with her until her very fate came to pass, and he himself would be struck by fate.

The audience, naturally, pressed for him to tell them the whole story of this mysterious Grusha, and Ivan Severyanych indulged them.

XV

You see, Ivan Severyanych began, my prince was good-hearted enough, but he was unsteady. Anything he wanted, he just had to have it immediately, and he'd go off his nut completely if he couldn't, nothing he wouldn't do for it – and then, when he finally got whatever it was, it never seemed to bring much happiness. That's exactly what had happened with this gypsy girl, and her – I mean Grusha's – father and his gang must've been able to tell who they were dealing with from the start, and had extracted such a price for her – a misjudgment of his estate, which, though imposing, was saddled with debts. To get his hands on the kind of money the gypsies were demanding, he'd had to take out loans and quit his post.

Knowing him as well as I did, I didn't expect much good for Grusha to come of the arrangement, and it didn't. At first he was very attentive, wouldn't let her out of his sight, waiting on her hand and foot, and then the yawns started creeping in, and he'd ask me to come along and round out the company.

"Come grab a seat," he'd say, "listen in."

So I would; I'd set a stool somewhere close to the doors and sit and listen. More often than not the same thing happened: he'd tell her to start singing and she'd scowl back. "Who should I sing to? she'd ask. You've grown so cold. I want my songs to torment somebody, burn up his soul."

So the prince would call me in, and the two of us would sit there and listen together, and it happened like this so much that after a while Grusha would remind him to call me in, and we got pretty chummy, so that it wasn't unusual that after she'd finished singing, she and the prince and I would take tea in their bedroom, except that I, of course, would always sit off at my own table, or else at the window-sill, except when she was alone, and then she always invited me to come sit next to her. A lot of time went by like that, the prince getting more and more worried all the time. One day he pulled me aside and said, "You know, Ivan Severyanov, things with me, they aren't too good."

"How do you mean? Thanks be to God, you live as you should, and you have what you need."

But somehow I'd offended him. "Is that right, my nearly-almost-fit-for-society friend? I have everything, do I? Well tell me, what do I *have*?"

"You have everything, sir, that you need."

"Oh, that's rich," he said. "I've grown so poor I have to crunch a list of numbers before I can get myself a bottle of table wine. Tell me – you call that living? Do you?"

"Aha," I thought, "so *that's* what you're so bent out of shape over," and I said, "Well, so what if you need to skip the wine from time to time? You've got something sweeter than wine, than honey."

He of course caught the allusion to Grusha, and it seemed to give him a pang of shame. At any rate, he started pacing back and forth, waving his arms all around.

"Yes, of course, of course, naturally.... it's just... I... I've been cooped up in this place so long, it's been ages since I saw an unfamiliar face...

"Strangers? What do you need strangers for? You're here with your heart's desire."

"Brother, you understand nothing. One's only good where there's another."

Aha, I thought. *This bird's changed his tune.*

"So what'll you do next?"

"Let's go into business," he said, leaning forward, "selling horses. I miss all those breeders and purchasers coming to my estate." Well, it's not very dignified work and it's unfit for a gentleman, but, I thought, "take things as they come," and I said, "Let's do it."

So we started up a little stable. Soon the prince had gotten totally carried away, as usual – no sooner had he put together a little cash than he'd go out and buy up some horses, any horse that struck him, ignoring my advice, so that the business came to nothing, all supply and no demand. It hardly even mattered, since all too soon he'd burned out on it and threw up his arms at the horse business, jumping to do anything else that popped into his head: one day there'd be some ingenious idea for a mill that he'd have constructed straight away, and the next he had a business plan and was opening a saddler's shop. All any of it ever came to was debts and losses, and, what was worse, a real downturn in his character. You'd hardly ever see him at home anymore, always flying here and there in hot pursuit of something or other, and Grusha would be left all alone, not to mention that she was, how to put it, with child. She was terribly lonesome, and she confessed to me that she rarely saw him. Still, she put a brave face on it and never let her desperation show, and once he'd been home for a day or two and started to grow restless, she'd always tell him, "Why don't you go and find some fun somewhere, my shimmering emerald? I can't expect to give you everything you need, simple and uneducated as I am."

That'd be all it took to fill him with shame. He'd take her hand and kiss it, and then stick it out for two or three more days, until he couldn't take it anymore and he'd bust out, leaving her in my care.

"You look after her, my half-lit, half-empty Ivan Severyanych. You're a real artist, not some wastrel like me, no, a true artist of the highest caliber, which is probably why you seem to know how to get along with her so well. As for me, I've had about enough of the 'shimmering emerald' crap."

"Oh, listen to you! How can you say such a thing? They're words of love!"

"Words of love they may be," he replied, "but tiresome, stupid garbage all the same."

I didn't say a word back, but from that moment on I made a point of running into her all the time. When the prince wasn't around, I'd come by twice a day with a tray of tea and try to make her smile. It seemed like she could use a smile, since every time we started talking she'd lash out with the most bitter complaints:

"My dear friend," she'd say, "my confidant Ivan Severyanych, bitter jealousy, my darling, is tormenting me."

Naturally, I did whatever I could to console her.

"Tormented?" I'd say. "What's to be tormented by – wherever he goes, he always comes home to you."

But she'd start crying and pounding her breast, and say, "No, my dear friend, stop protecting me, I must know: Where does he go?"

"He passes time with other gentlemen in the neighborhood, or else he heads into town."

"And you're sure he hasn't got another girl somewhere? Maybe there's someone he was in love with long before meeting me that he's gone back to, and now he'll drop me and run off with her?" And at the thought of it such a fire tore through her eyes that I started feeling really afraid even to look at her.

While I was comforting her, I thought, *Who even knows what he's up to?* – he wasn't too regular a presence, if you take my meaning. But once the thought that he might marry took hold of her, she wouldn't let it alone: "Oh, take a little ride into town, oh, my darling Ivan Severyanych, oh won't you please? Go and nose around a little till you get the story on him, then come back and give it to me straight. She just wouldn't stop badgering me to do it, till finally I thought, *Alright, alright, I'll go and have a look, come what may. But if I find out he's been unfaithful, I won't tell her everything. Still, it'll be helpful to bring matters out into the light of day.*

So I cooked up a story about needing to stop by the herb-sellers' stall and pick up some medicine for the horses, and I headed off – not so very casually, mind you, but with a pretty clever ruse in mind.

Grusha had no idea, and the Prince was strict as could be that nobody tell her, that before he met her he'd had another love in town – a certain Yevgenia Semyonovna, daughter of a government secretary. She was known all over town as a master pianist and a great lady besides, not half bad-looking either, but then she'd put on a lot of weight, which, if the rumors were to be believed, was why he'd left her. But even so, he'd bought her and their daughter a house, things being flush at the time, and they lived on whatever money it brought in. As for him, though, he stopped coming round to see Yevgenia Semyonovna just as soon as she'd moved into the house he bought her. But some of the servants from the household kept coming by for old times' sake when they were in town, since she'd always been so kindly and sweet to us all and was always just dying to know what the prince had been up to.

So as soon as I hit town I headed straight to see the dear Baronness, and I said, "My dearest Yevgenia Semyonovna, I've come to ask if I can stay with you."

"Of course. I'm very pleased to see you. I'm just surprised that you're here instead of at the prince's apartment.'

"Are you telling me the prince has an apartment in town?"

"Yes, of course. He's been living here for more than a week, starting up some kind of a business here."

"You don't say, ma'am. Tell me, what sort of a business?"

"A cotton mill," she answered.

"My Lord! What'll he think of next?!"

"What's wrong with that?"

"Oh, not a thing," I said, "not a thing. I'm just surprised is all."

She gave a little smile. "If it's a surprise you want, then I've got a better one: the prince has just written to say he's coming by today. I gather he wants to get a look at his daughter."

"Are you going to let him in, matushka?"

She shrugged. "Sure, why not? If that's what he wants, let him come see his little girl." As she said it she sighed and stared off into her thoughts, head drooped, looking still so young and so composed and lily-white, and she carried herself in such a way, I mean, if you compared her with Grusha… oh, Grusha, the best polish she could put on herself was that oh-my-precious-emerald business. I became filled with indignation on Grusha's behalf.

Oh, I thought. *I only hope his eye doesn't stray from his daughter, I can just see you catching the gaze of that insatiable heart of his! Nothing good could come of that for my Grushenka.* With this running through my head I went into the nursery, where Yevgenia Semyonovna had ordered the nurse to pour me a cup of tea.

A call at the front door. I heard the housemaid come running up gleefully and announce to the nurse, "That dear prince is here!" At this I stood up to head into the kitchen. But this old biddy nurse – a certain Tatyana Yakovlevna from around Moscow – what a blabbermouth! When you're addicted to gossip, there's nothing scarier than losing your audience, and she got right in my way: "Oh, don't go, Mister Ivan Headanovsky! Let's we two duck into the dressing room, cop a squat behind the wardrobe. She'll never bring him in there, and we've got so much to talk about, you and me!"

I said yes, hoping this Tatyana Yakovlevna would let slip something that Grusha could use, and then we just stood there a minute, I with my tea and a little eau-de-Cologne bottle of rum that Yevgenia Semyonovna had had brought along with it, and since I was sworn off drink anyway, I thought, Well, maybe if I slipped a little to the old lady – oh, bless her heart! – maybe it'd loosen her up a little, really get her talking, and so, when she looked away, I poured it into her teacup.

We snuck out of the nursery and took our seats behind the wardrobe, in what wasn't a room so much as a long hallway with a door at one end, a door that, as luck would have it, led right into the room where Yevgenia Semyonovna had received the prince, which was in fact right next to the couch they were sitting on. Maybe they thought that locked door with the rug hung over one side gave them privacy, but from where I was sitting I could hear everything they said, just as though we were in the same room.

The prince burst in. "Hello, my dear old friend!" he said.

"How do you do, Prince? To what do I owe the honor?"

"We can talk about it later, my dear. First let me have a look at you, let me give you a kiss," and I could hear him plant one and then start asking after his daughter. Yevgenia Semyonovna let him know that she was in the house.

"Is she well?"

"Well enough."

"I imagine she's grown, eh?"

Yevgenia Semyonovna let out a chortle and answered, "Yes, of course she's grown."

"Could I see her?"

"Why, gladly," she said, and as she got up to walk into the nursery and call that nanny, Tatyana Yakovlevna, the one I was busy having such a grand old time with.

"Oh, nurse," she called out, "bring little Lyudochka to see the prince!"

Tatyana Yakovlevna spat, set her saucer on the table, and said, "What a pain! A person can't sit down and have a nice chat around here, she can't! Nothing you won't spoil, is there?!" and she quickly grabbed some of the baronness's skirts off the wall and draped them over me and told me to keep put, and skulked off after the little girl. I stayed behind by the wardrobe, and I could hear him kissing her again and again, twirling her around on his knees, and then he asked, "Would you like to go for a ride in my carriage, *mon enfant*?"

She didn't say a word. He turned to Yevgenia Semyonovna. "*Je vous prie*," he said, "please, let her take a ride in my carriage with the nurse." She said something back in French, oh you know, how come and *pourquoi*, all that, but he muttered something to the effect that it was "absolutely imperative" that she go, and after going around like this for a minute, Yevgenia Semyonovna must've agreed, and she told the nurse, "Have her dressed and take her for a ride."

They went out, leaving mother and father all alone, just the two of them, and me of course, listening from behind the wardrobe. After all, it's hardly as though I could leave. Besides, I thought to myself, *Finally I can get a close look what's going on here. I wonder what dreadful plans they might have for my Grusha?*

XVI

No sooner had I made up my mind to eavesdrop than I became dissatisfied: I didn't just want to listen, I wanted to look on, too, to see them with my own eyes, and that didn't turn out to be too hard. I climbed up onto a stool as quietly as I could and examined the doorway till I found a little ding where the door groove was missing. I thrust a greedy eye against it, and I could see them in there – the prince on the couch, the baroness standing by the window, it seemed watching her little girl get into the carriage.

After it had driven off, she turned to him and said, "Prince, I've done everything you asked. Now tell me, what brings you here?"

"Damn what brings me here! It's not a bear, it won't scamper off into the wood. Come over here first, get close to me and we'll talk, like it was in the old days."

The Baroness just stood there with her brow furrowed, leaning on the window, not saying a word. The prince got even more agitated, "What's gotten into you? I'll say it again, I need to talk to you."

She relented. When he saw that she was listening, his mood was brightened immediately.

"Yes, yes that's right, my dear, you come have a seat here, yes, just like in the old days," and he tried to get his arms around her. She pushed him away.

"What business brings you here, Prince? What is your concern? What can I do for you?"

"My goodness," he asked, "do you expect me to just launch right into it without any pleasantries?"

"I certainly do. Tell me right now, what brings you here? We've known each other a little while now – no need to stand on ceremony."

"I need money," the prince said. She eyed him silently. "Not a lot of money," he added.

"Oh? How much?"

"Just twenty thousand for now."

She again said nothing, and the prince went on, painting quite a picture "You see, I'm buying a cotton mill, and I haven't got a penny right now. But when I buy it, of course, I'll be a millionaire! I'm going to change everything – scrap the old equipment and replace it, then start churning out scarves in bright colors to sell to the Asiatics at the Makaryev Fair outside Nizhny. I'll make them out of anything, garbage, whatever – you dye it the right colors and they lose their minds to buy them. We won't be able to keep inventory in the shops! But for now I need twenty thousand as a deposit on the factory."

Yevgenia Semyonovna looked up: "But where will you get that kind of cash?"

"I couldn't tell you that myself. But get it I must, and once I do I've got everything figured out. I know this guy, Ivan the Head, an army connoisseur, awfully dumb but a hell of a fellow – honest and trustworthy, even lived with Asiatics as their prisoner and knows them inside and out. Right now while the Makaryev Fair is up I'll send The Head with some samples to make a few deals, drum up some business, then – and first thing – I'll pay back that twenty thousand…"

He fell silent, and the aroness stayed silent a while, until finally with a sigh she began, "Your plan, Prince, is perfect."

"Wouldn't you say?"

"I would, I would. Here's what you'll do: put down a deposit on this factory, at which point everyone immediately regards you as a manufacturer, of course. And then all the society people will start to gossip about how well you're doing…"

"Precisely!"

"Yes, and then…"

"And then The Head will pick up so much business at the Makaryev that I'll pay you back and grow rich!"

"Please do not interrupt me. First, you get the Chairman of the Bureau of Nobles all buttered up, then, while he still thinks you're rich, you marry his daughter. And then, what do you know, you really are rich. As long as you didn't forget to secure to a dowry."

"Is that what you think?"

"Is there something else to think?"

"If you've got it all figured out just like that, God grant that we all sip honey through your lips."

"*We?*"

"Of course," he said. "Things'll be great by then. You'll mortgage the house for me, and I'll pay your daughter back ten thousand interest on the twenty thousand.."

"The house is yours: you gave it to her, and you can take it if you want."

He started to object. "No, no. That is, it's… not mine. You are her mother, so I must ask you… of course, you should certainly not agree, if I don't have your trust…"

"Oh, *entirely*, Prince, how *entirely* you have my trust. Why, I've even trusted you with my life, and with my honor."

"Oh, yes, yes, about that… Well, thank you for that… kindness, yes. So I'll have the mortgage papers sent over tomorrow, for your signature?"

"Send them. I'll sign."

"Aren't you worried?"

"No, no. After everything I've lost, nothing can worry me."

"Can't you feel a little sorry for me? Come on, can't you? Don't you still love me just the tiniest bit? Or at least feel pity for me? Don't you?"

She laughed out loud. "Entirely, Prince, but talk is cheap. Come on, wouldn't you rather just have some cloudberry preserves? They're perfectly in season."

He seemed, at last, to get the point: this was not the conversation he'd been anticipating. He stood up and forced a smile.

"No, eat the cloudberries yourself. I've lost the taste. I thank you kindly, I'll take my leave," and as he leaned in to kiss her hand the carriage pulled up outside.

Yevgenia Semyonovna, as she was waving good-bye, asked, "Oh, and what will you do with your black-eyed little gypsy?"

He slapped his forehead and cried out, "Oh, yes of course, her! You're such a clever woman! Believe it or not, I think about how clever you are all the time. Oh, *thank* you, darling, for reminding me about that shimmering ruby of mine."

"You just forgot about her altogether?"

"I swear to God I forgot. Out of sight, out of mind! I'll have to make some arrangements for the little fool."

"I'd make those arrangements carefully," Yevgenia Semyonovna said, glaring at him. "Look, she's no Russian, some mixture of mild blood and fresh milk. She's not going to let you run off with peaceful resignation – she'll never forgive what you've done to her."

"I'm sure she will."

"Is she in love with you, Prince? People say she's deeply in love with you."

"The thrill's gone. But thank God she and The Head are great friends.

"What good does that do you?" Yevgenia Semyonovna asked.

"Not a thing! I'll just buy them a house, register Ivan as a merchant, and they can get married and start a life together."

Yevgenia Semyonovna just shook her head with a smirk. "Oh, my prince, my prince, my idiotic little prince. Have you no conscience?"

"Leave my conscience alone, please. I swear to God I'm in no mood for it. I need to see Ivan The Head immediately, today if possible."

The baroness told him that Ivan The Head was in town, and was in fact staying with her. The prince was extremely glad and asked her to send me to see him as soon as possible, and then left immediately.

After that, everything seemed to happen in the way of a fairy tale. The prince loaded me up with writs and certificates to the effect that he was a factory owner, and he taught me how to talk about the kinds of cloth he produced, and sent me from town straight to the Makaryev, so that I didn't even have time to make a stop and see Grusha, and for the whole trip I was peeved at the prince – how could he say that she'd be my wife? At the Makaryev I struck paydirt. I got orders from the Asiatics there, and money, and patterns. I immediately forwarded the money on to the prince, and then came back, to an estate that I couldn't even recognize! It was as though a sorcerer had transformed it. It was decorated like, well, a peasant's cottage decked out for the holidays, and the wing where Grusha had lived was gone without a trace – bulldozed in fact, and replaced by a new one. I gasped and shouted out for my little Grusha, but no one could tell me a thing about her: all the servants were new, such smug little snoots that not one of them would show me in to see the prince. Before this we'd been thick as war buddies, everything so simple between us, but now everything had lots of formalities, and if I wanted to say something to the prince I had to say it through his personal valet.

I've never had any patience for that sort of thing, and I don't think I would've stayed another minute if not for poor Grusha. No matter what I did, I just couldn't seem to find out what had happened to her. When I asked the older servants, they wouldn't say a word to me – clearly they'd been warned not to. Finally, I pushed through and got one of the old maids to let loose. My Grushenka had been here until not long ago, ten days now since she took that carriage ride with the prince and didn't come back. I asked the coachmen who'd driven them – they stonewalled me. All they'd say was that the prince had changed to hired horses at the first stop, and sent the old ones back while he rode off with Grusha, no one knew where. No matter how I searched, there was no trace of her. That was that. he'd dug a knife into her, the scum, or else shot her and buried the body in a ditch in the woods and covered it with dry leaves after, or drowned her... in the throes of his passions he was capable of anything. After all, she really was in the way of his getting married, since Yevgenia Semyonovna had spoken the truth: Grusha was in love with him, the cur, with all the wildfire of her unruly gypsy heart, and it wasn't in her to submit in the face of his shenanigans the way that Yevgenia Semyonovna, that good Christian woman, had done, letting her life dissipate into his like lamplight into an ikon.

It was easy enough to imagine how it must've happened: he'd tell her all about his wedding plans, and, a raging inferno tearing over her, she'd explode into curses and threats. He'd put an end to her right there.

The more I considered it, the surer I felt that this was the only way it could've happened. I couldn't stomach watching the preparations for his marriage to the chairman's daughter. When the big day finally came, and all the maids were given brightly printed kerchiefs to wear, and all the men new liveries, one to correspond to the duties of every man, I wouldn't wear mine – I hid it all in my storeroom in the stables and set off for a walk in the woods, and stayed out till nightfall, never knowing where I was going, but just wondering with each step whether I'd come upon her murdered body. Evening fell and I left the woods, sat myself down on the steep bank of a stream, from where I could see the prince's house across the water, all lit up, wild with celebration, guests dancing around, music thundering out so loud you could hear it all the way over. I sat there, my thoughts drifting, until my gaze was fixed not on the house itself but on the water, where the light was reflected in the streaming current and the columns of the house rippling and waving like the pillars of some mansion in the sea. I felt so miserably forlorn, so howling with pain, that I did something I had never done even in all my years as a prisoner. I started talking to an unseen power, and, just like in the fairy tale about the brother who cried out for his sister, I called out for my Grunyushka, my ill-fated darling, in a voice that ached upon the waters, "Oh my little sister, oh my Grunyushka! Come to me, answer me! Come to me, appear before me for just one minute!"

And, what do you know. I wailed out that way three times, and then something terrifying happened. I could feel someone running toward me. I felt this person running around me in circles, whispering into my ear, staring me in the face, and then something started to materialize out of the darkness! The next thing I knew it had hung itself around my neck, convulsing…

XVII

This scared me so bad that I nearly fell over. Somehow, I held it together, and I could feel something lively and light around me, like a wounded crane, beating and sighing and not saying a word.

I made a silent prayer and – wait, what's this? – before my eyes I saw a vision of Grusha's face .

"My darling!" I cried. "My beloved! Do you still breathe, or have you come from the other side? You be straight with me, my poor waif, I don't fear death and I won't fear you either way."

She breathed and breathed the deepest sigh from her breast and said, "I'm alive."

"Oh, thank the Lord, thank the Lord."

"But I've come here to die."

"Listen to you," I said. "Grunyushka, God walks with you – how could you want to die? Let's run away and be together. We could have a happy life – I'll find a job somewhere, my sweet, and build a house for you. You could live with me there like a beloved sister."

"No, Ivan Severyanych, you gentle man, no, I can't. You're so tender-hearted! I'll always be grateful for your kindness. But as for me, I'm nothing but a wretched gypsy, and I can't go on. If I do I risk ruining an innocent soul.

"Who are you talking about? Whose soul are you pitying like this?"

"Hers, the young wife of my seducer. She's so young, so innocent, and my jealous heart will never let her alone. I just know that I'll kill her and myself."

"Don't say that! Cross yourself, quickly. My goodness, you are baptized, aren't you? Think of your soul!"

"Ha! I don't care for my soul at all. Let it go right to Hell. Here it's worse than Hell!"

I could see the poor woman was beside herself, no idea what she was saying. I took her hand and held it, and stared into her eyes. She was horribly changed. I couldn't stop wondering where all her beauty had gone. Even her body had withered away to nearly nothing, and just one eye shone from her dark face like a wolf's in the night, twice as big as it had been, her belly straining forward with all the months of pregnancy, almost to term now, her sweet face curled and hardened into a fist, black locks brushing her cheeks. I looked at her dress, a cheap cotton number, worn full of holes, no socks under her shoes.

"Tell me," I said breathlessly, "where did you come here from? Where have you been, and what happened to your looks?"

She broke into a wild grin and said, "What, am I not beautiful?! I am beautiful! I am beautiful! This is how my gentle lover repays my love, my faithful love, for loving him more than a woman ever loved him, forgetting my other lovers for him, out of my mind and out of all reason, yes, for all this he put me under lock and key and set guards on me, all just to protect my beauty…"

She exploded into wild cackles and, seething, she cried out, "Ach, curse your idiotic princely head! You think a gypsy girl's going to sit her life away in jail like one of your noble ladies? If I wanted I could go right up to that young wife of yours and gnaw out her throat with my teeth!"

She was careening into a fit of uncontrolled jealousy. I thought maybe I should try distracting her not with the fear of Hell, but by laying down a little sweet talk about the old days.

"Think of how he used to love you. I've never seen a guy in love like that! How he'd kiss your feet, kneel in front of the couch while you sang, kissing your scarlet slippers all over…"

I was beginning to get through to her, her black lashes quivering over dry cheeks, and looking out at the water she said in a hollow, small voice, "Loved me. Loved me, the bastard, loved me, loved me with perfect happiness as long as I didn't love him back. As soon as I fell for him – he left me. And for who? What, is she better than me, this other woman? Does she love him more? He is an ass, a perfect ass! Ah, but a winter's sun can't outburn summer's. In a hundred years, no one'll love him as I did. You tell him that, you tell him Grusha had a vision when she died, before she fell to the rocks."

I was glad she was talking again, and I kept her at it. "What is it that finally happened between you? What's the cause of all this?"

She threw up her hands. "Nothing but betrayal, pure and simple. He stopped liking me one day, just like that," and then, wouldn't you know, just as she's saying it she starts weeping. "He'd buy me dresses, whatever he liked, all these dresses with narrow waists, and I'd try to wear them to please him, but he'd just get mad, 'Take it off, it looks awful on you,' or then I'd come out in something looser but he'd get even angrier. 'Do you have any idea what you look like?' And I knew then that I'd lost him forever. I disgusted him…"

With this she burst out into inconsolable blubbering. Looking straight off into space, she went on in a whisper, "I… sensed it for a long time, that he was getting sick of me. But I wanted to see his conscience. I thought, "Just don't badger him, don't pester" – I appealed to his pity, and he pitied me."

Then she gave me the story of the last time she'd seen the prince, something so idiotic I couldn't believe it then and still can't. What kind of a scoundrel would turn his back on a woman forever over such a thing?

XVIII

Grusha told me everything. "After you up and vanished," – that is, after I'd been dispatched to the Makaryev – "the prince went away for a long time, and talk started to reach me that he was getting married. I cried and cried over him, and lost my looks… my heart ached for it, and I could feel our child kicking inside me. I thought: *it'll die in my womb*. Then, one day, I suddenly heard them break out into whispers of "He's coming!" I started quivering and ran to my quarters to get gussied up for him, threw on my emerald earrings and pulled out his favorite dress, a blue one trimmed in lace with a low bodice. I was so flustered from zipping around that I couldn't get the back fastened, so I threw on a crimson shawl to cover it and raced to the front steps, all trembling and stumbling over myself while I shouted, "My darling, my darling, my true one, my sparkling emerald!" and I threw myself around his neck and fainted."

She looked nauseated just thinking about it.

"I came to on the sofa in my room, struggling to

remember whether it had all really happened or been just a dream. All I knew was that I was terribly weak, and I didn't see him for a long time. I'd send and send for him, but he just never came."

Then finally one day he did, and I said, "Well, finally! I was starting to think you'd forgotten all about me."

"I'm a busy man."

"Busy? But what's got you so busy? You weren't before, my shimmering emerald!" I reached out my arms to embrace him, but he just grimaced back and yanked the ribbon around my neck as hard as he could.

"Thank goodness the silk was all frayed and weak so the ribbon tore – otherwise, he would've strangled me, which I think is what he was trying to do, because while he did it he went white as a sheet and hissed at me, "How can you wear such a filthy ribbon?"

"What do you care about my ribbon? If you must know, it used to be clean, but I'm so frightfully melancholy and lonesome all the time that I sweat terribly."

He spat three times and left, left and went out, and came back still seething just before evening. "Let's go for a carriage ride!" He made a big show of treating me gently, even kissed me on the head. I climbed in with him, not suspecting a thing, and we rode off. We rode for a long time, had to change the horses twice. I didn't want to pester him about where we were headed, but as the scenery changed I knew it was somewhere swampy and wooded, horrible and savage. There, in the middle of the woods, we arrived at some kind of a beehive, and behind the beehive was a little house. Three girls came out, young, strong girls in bright red dresses, calling me ma'am. No sooner had I stepped out of the coach than they grabbed me under the arms and carried me inside to a room that had been all made up.

"Something was fishy right away, especially with those serving-girls. My heart sank."

"What is this," I asked him. "What kind of a place are we in?"

"This is your new home."

I started weeping, kissing his hand, desperately begging him not to leave me there, but his heart was hard: he shoved me away and left.

At this poor little Grushenka paused and bent her face down with a heavy sigh. She went on: "I wanted to leave! I tried a hundred escapes in vain: those girls didn't blink an eye or let me alone for a second. I rotted away like that for a while. Then I hatched a little plan: I pretended my spirits had taken a turn for the better and skipped around like I hadn't a care in the world. I said I wanted to go out for a stroll and they let me, their gazes fixed on me like ice. While I strolled I studied the position of the trees, how they branched over the sky and what their bark was like, how the noon sun struck them, everything. Then yesterday I made my move. After lunch I went out to the meadow with them and said, "Sweeties! Who's up for some blind man's buff?"

They said alright.

"Only instead of blindfolds, let's tie our hands behind our backs. We can tag each other with our bottoms."

They said alright to that too.

So we did. I tied up the first girl's hands, oh very snugly, oh yes! The next one dashed off and I tackled her behind a bush. The third ran off screaming, but I wrestled her down there in front of the other two. Pregnant as I am I dashed off into the woods faster than a racehorse, leaving the three of them all tied up and screaming. Oh, how I ran and I ran, all through the woods, all night long, until the sun came up and I collapsed by some old beehives in a clearing. A little old man came up to me, spoke in mumbles I couldn't make sense of. He seemed made of beeswax, and he reeked of honey and there were bees swarming around in his yellow eyebrows. I told him that I was trying to find you, Ivan Severyanych, and he said, "Call to him, maiden, once into the wind, and once against it: he'll grow lonely for you and come track you down where you are." He gave me some drinking water and a little meal of honey and cucumbers. I drank and ate and then headed off again, calling for you just like he'd told me, into the wind and then against it – and look! Here you are! It worked." She threw her arms around me and started kissing me and said, "You're just like a darling brother to me."

"And you're like a dear sister to me," I said, and it was so overwhelming that I started to cry too.

"Oh, Ivan Severyanych, I've known all along that you alone loved me truly. My tender-hearted friend, my darling. Show that you love me one last time, do please what I ask in this fateful hour!"

"Tell me: what do you want?"

"No," she said," not until you promise you'll do it, no matter how terrible." I swore on my soul's salvation that I would. "Not enough! You'd let yourself be damned for my sake, I know it. Do better, make some even more terrible oath!"

"I can't even think of one."

"I've got one for you. Now just repeat whatever I say immediately, without thinking." I stupidly agreed to this, and she went on, "Damn my soul, just as you damn your own, if you don't keep your word."

"Very well," I said. "I damn our souls both."

"Good, now listen closely. You can be my soul's very savior. I can't go on like this, torturing myself with his unfaithfulness in plain view. I have no strength left to bear his outrages. If I live one day more, I'll do the both of them in, and if I start to feel bad for them then I'll kill myself too and damn my soul forever. Oh, please take pity on me, my beloved, my darling little brother, please put a knife in my heart!"

I started backing away, hurriedly making cross after cross in the air, but she threw herself at my feet, bawling, arms wrapped around my knees, begging me, "Don't you see? You'll go on living, you can make peace with God and pray for me! Please, don't leave, don't make me do it myself!"

"I, I just, well I…"

Ivan Severyanych furrowed his brow and gnawed at his whiskers, not so much speaking as sighing out from the depths of his tormented breast. "She got the knife out of my pocket… opened the blade… put it… in my hand…

and just to see her like that… the pain… it was too much to bear…"

"If you don't kill me I'll teach you all a lesson, I'll become the lowest kind of a tramp," she said.

I couldn't stop shaking, told her to say her prayers. I couldn't stab her, I couldn't. So I threw her from the lip of the ravine all the way down into the river."

Having heard all this, we started to doubt Ivan Severyanych for the first time, and there was a long silence, broken eventually when someone cleared his throat and said, "And she drowned?"

"Straight to the bottom," Ivan Severyanych answered.

"And afterward?"

"How do you mean?"

"Well, you must've suffered, eh?"

"What do you think."

XIX

I ran from there as fast as I could, no thought to where I was headed, and all I remember is, I could hear some-one coming up behind me, horribly tall and big, shameless, naked, his body all black with a little head like an onion bulb, hair all over him, and I thought, *if this isn't Cain it's the Beast himself*, and I ran and ran and called on my guardian angel. The next thing I knew I was by the side of a highway somewhere, sitting under a bent old willow. Perfect autumn day – sun shining, a cold wind stirring up dust and whirls of yellow leaves. I didn't know what time it was, or where I was, or where the road before me led, with nothing in my heart, nothing at all, no feelings, no idea what to do. All I could think about was Grusha's slaughtered soul, and my responsibility to keep her out of hell with my sufferings. But how to go about doing it was another story – I didn't know, and it filled me with despair. Then suddenly some-thing touched me on the shoulder, a dead willow branch that snapped off and was snatched into the wind, rolling down a long way, and as I followed it, I saw – Grusha was there, but as a little girl, not more than six or seven, with little wings growing out from behind her shoulders. No sooner had I spotted her than she zipped off, a stir of dust and fallen leaves swirling in her wake.

I thought: *that can only be her soul, following faithfully where I go to show me the way.* I left. The whole day I walked on, not knowing where I was headed, exhausted till I nearly collapsed, and then some people came up on me from behind, an old couple in a two-horse carriage, and said, "Come in, you poor man, let us give you a lift." I did. We all rode on. You could see there was something eating at them.

"What a mess we're in! Our son's been conscripted, and we can't afford to hire someone to replace him."

I felt sorry for the little old couple. "I'd do it for free, but I haven't got papers."

"Don't worry about that, we'll handle it. You just have to start going by his name, Pyotr Serdyukov."

"Sure, what do I care? As long as I can still pray to my protector Saint John the Baptist, call me anything you want."

So that was that, and they took me to the recruitment office of another city, gave me twenty-five rubles in silver, and promised to keep helping me the rest of their lives. I gave the money to a poor monastery for Grusha's soul and petitioned the authorities to send me to the Caucasus, where I could die most quickly for my faith. This was granted, and I lived more than fifteen years in the Caucasus without ever giving away my real name or identity, doing everything under the name Pyotr Serdyukov, and praying for myself only on the feast day of Saint John, through the intermediary of the Blessed Evangelist. I forgot all about my life before the army, and it was in my last year of service, on Saint John's day of all days, that we had to chase a band of Tatars we'd been having trouble with across the River Koysa. There's a few different rivers called Koysa around there: the one that runs through Lydia is called the Andian Koysa, the one that traverses Avaria they call the Avarian Koysa, and then there's the Korikumuian and Kuzikumuian Koysas, all of them flowing together and feeding into the River Sulak. All four are swift and cold, but especially the Andian, the one those blasted Tatars had skulked across. We'd butchered more of those Tatars than we could count, but the ones who'd survived and made it across were sitting on the opposite shore behind some boulders, and the very instant we showed ourselves they'd fire at us. There was slyness in how they shot at us – a Tatar would never pull the trigger until he was sure he had a perfect shot, and this made the most of the powder they had, which was a lot less than ours, so that even when we were standing right out in front of them the bastards wouldn't fire. Our colonel, a man of great verve, fancied himself another Suvorov, and was always adding the words "Lord have mercy" to whatever he said. The example of his bravery gave us all courage. He sat down on the little bank, dangling his bare feet into the freezing water, bragging, "Lord have mercy, if this water isn't just as warm as a bucket of milk right out of the udder! Which one of you sportsmen, you heroes, is going to swim across with a rope so we can get a bridge built?"

With the colonel sitting there chatting with us like that, the Tatars poked the barrels of two rifles out though a gap in the rock, and held their fire. As soon as two volunteers had dived into the Koysa, shots rang out and they sank like stones. Another two immediately jumped in and we tore loose against the Tatars, but they just hopped back behind their rocks, which was all we could hit, leaving them, the hideous demons, with free rein over the water, which soon went red with blood. A third pair didn't make it halfway. The sight of this really thinned out the "sportsmen" from the crowd, who could all see that this had gone from warfare to outright slaughter. Still, the dogs were howling for justice. The colonel said, "Listen up, heroes! Maybe one of you has a… a mortal sin on his conscience? Lord have mercy, what a great opportunity this is for a man like that to have his lawlessness washed away by his blood!"

I thought, *Well what am I waiting for, am I going to have a better shot than this? Oh glory, oh bless the Lord – my hour at last!* and I stepped forward, said an Our Father, lowered myself to the ground in every direction before my comrades and superiors, and said to myself, "Well, Grusha, sister of my heart, accept my blood for your sins!" With that, I bit down on the string tied to one end of the rope, took a running start, and plunged into the water.

It was ungodly cold. I started cramping up everywhere, a stab under my arms, explosion in my chest, legs pulling down, but I just kept swimming. Our bullets were soaring overhead, and all around me the Tatars' were plunging through in straight lines. I couldn't tell whether I'd been wounded, but the next thing I knew, there I was on the opposite shore. From there the Tatars couldn't kill me – I was positioned behind the wall of a gorge, and to angle toward me they'd have to step into the hail of bullets our boys didn't stop sending from the opposite bank. I just stood there, under the rocks, pulling the whole length of the rope across foot by foot, and when I'd finished they drew the bridge over and they had crossed it before I knew what hit me. Me, I was just standing there, completely lost in wonder, because had anybody seen what I'd seen? What I'd seen while I was swimming was Grusha, flying over me, she looked about sixteen now, and her wings had grown huge, shimmering across the whole width of the river, protecting me like a force field. When I saw that no one else mentioned this, I thought I'd better keep it to myself. The colonel put his arms around me and gave me a kiss, praising me in front of everyone, "Lord have mercy! That's some fine work there, Pyotr Serdyukov, some fine work!"

"Your High Nobleness, it was no fine work at all. It just proves what a terrible sinner I am – neither the earth nor the waters will take me."

"Terrible sinner you say? What was your terrible sin?"

"I've taken a great many innocent lives in my day," I said, and then I went on to tell him stories all night long, there in his tent, everything I'm telling you now.

He listened with great patience, pondered what I'd told him a while, and then he said, "Lord have mercy, what a burden you've borne! And all by yourself, too. Well, brother, all the same I'm recommending you for an officer's commission. I'll send my recommendation tomorrow."

"As you wish, but shouldn't you also send over an inquiry as to whether or not I really did murder that gypsy girl?"

"Alright," he said. "I'll make the inquiry."

And so he did, but when the report came on his inquiry it said that I'd been lying. It explained that "we have no record of any event with a gypsy girl, and although an Ivan Severyanyeh did serve in the prince's employ, he was later emancipated and died in the house of a certain Serdyukov family, servants to the Crown."

What else could I possibly do to prove my guilt?

The colonel just said, "Brother, don't you lie to me again! Must be all that cold water and fear scrambled your brains a little. I'm glad for you, that what you said isn't true. Now there's nothing to stand between you and being an officer, Lord have a mercy, and that's good news."

I was starting to get a little shaken up at this point: had I really shoved Grusha into the water, or was it all a mad dream I'd cooked up in my desperation to see her?

For my bravery I was made an officer, but since I insisted on sticking to the truth, on opening the secrets of my wayward life to everyone, they got rid of me soon thereafter: said they wished for me a life free of worry, shoved a Saint George Cross in my hand, and pushed me along into resigning my commission.

"Please accept our congratulations," the colonel told me. "You are hereby admitted to the nobility and may work in the civil service. Lord have mercy, what an easy life you'll lead from here on out," and he gave me a letter to pass along to a big man in Petersburg. "Track him down," he told me, "he'll set you up with a career and look after you." And I did make it to Piter with the letter, but it didn't bring me any career luck.

"Why not?"

"I went around for a long time without a position. And then I fell in with *fita*, and everything got even worse."

"You fell in with *fita*? What does that mean?"

"The man I'd been sent to, a big boss out there, set me up with a post as an information clerk at the Registration Office. Every clerk is assigned his own letter, and he handles the case of everyone whose name starts with it. Some letters are very good, like B, or P, or K – a lot of last names begin with them, so the clerks assigned to them pull in a good living. But me they stuck with *fita*. Fita! The most unimportant letter, which practically nothing begins with. Even when someone's name does start with it they're always trying to wriggle and writhe free: they come in to register themselves as noblemen and just spell out their names with an F. There you are, spinning your wheels around to find him under fita, and meanwhile he's registered himself with the F guy. You can't make a living off of fita, not hardly. So seeing how bad my prospects were, I tried to find work as a coachman, like in the old days. No one was hiring. "You're a nobleman, an officer," they'd say, "a holder of military honors – how could we curse at you, or beat you bloody?" I came damn close to hanging myself in those days, for the desperation I walked around feeling. Thank God I didn't! Instead I thought to save myself from starving by taking work as an artist."

"What kind of an artist?'

"An actor, actually."

"In what theater?"

"A sideshow on Admiralty Square. They were alright with the nobility and everyone was welcome there: officers, civil servants, students, and especially a lot of visitors from the Governing Senate."

"And did you like your life there?"

"No sir, I did not."

"Why not?"

"Well, first of all, we had to memorize our lines and rehearse during Holy Week and Maslenitsa, right when they're singing 'Open, Ye Gates of Penance," in church. And second of all, the part they gave me was awfully burdensome."

"What was it?"

"I played Satan."

"What was so difficult about that?"

"I'll tell you what. For one thing, there were two interludes I had to dance in, and I was supposed to do a series of somersaults, which was especially miserable in my costume, a full-body goatskin covered in wool with a long wire tail that was always tangling itself up in my legs, plus two horns on my head that would catch or even rip any damned thing you left on the stage with them; besides, I was no spring chicken anymore, and had lost a lot of my grace, plus, according to the script, my character was to spend the entire production being beaten. All in all, a miserable situation. Miserable even though the sticks weren't real – they were canvas tubes stuffed with some flaky substance, but still, it became unendurable, getting hit with these things all day, and some of the actors, I don't know whether it was to keep warm or just to have a little fun, took to hitting me pretty hard. The ones from the Senate were worst of all – they seemed quite experienced and comfortable with this. They're a real clique, and the chance to put one over on an army man was more than they could resist. So they'd cut loose and they were just monsters, really, beating me from noon, when the police flag would go up, straight until midnight, smashing me endlessly for the crowd's amusement. Nothing good ever happened for me there. And on top of that, there was a bit of an incident, and I was forced to quit my role."

"An incident? What happened?"

"I boxed a prince's ear."

"A prince? Who?"

"Not a real one – an actor playing a prince: one of the senate guys, the Collegiate Secretary."

"What did you hit him for?"

"Because he had it coming. A nasty little buffoon he was, a dreamer who spent all his time dreaming to come up with practical jokes at the expense of others.

"You mean your expense?"

"Oh me too, for sure. Always playing pranks on me. Like, in the rehearsal room where we'd sit around some coals to take tea, he'd sneak up behind me and pin my tail to the horns or do some other stupid thing that I wouldn't notice until I was out in front of the public, and then the manager would get mad at me. Now, myself, I could take that kind of hazing no problem. But then one day he started bothering one of our fairies. She was just a girl from a nobleman's family fallen on hard times, playing the goddess Fortuna, who had to rescue this prince from my clutches. For her role she had to wear a shimmering tulle dress with wings, and that winter was so harsh that her poor little hands would go quite blue, and cramp up, and he was always bothering her and pawing at her, until finally one time, when we'd all gone through a trapdoor together at the climax of the show, he started pinching her all over. That was it: I beat the pinch right out of him."

"How did that turn out?'

"It was fine. The only witness down there was that little fairy, so nothing would have come of it except that all the Senate men went into an uproar and demanded that I be kicked out of the company. The manager would've done anything to make them happy. He kicked me out in a second."

"Where did you go after that?"

"I was left with nothing to eat and no place to lay my head, but that little fairy would bring me food sometimes. After a while it felt scandalous, though, that she, this poor little fairy, hard as she worked, should have to take care of me, so I thought and thought, racked my brains day and night, trying to come up with a way out of this situation. I didn't want to turn back to my old friend fita, and besides, some other poor guy would have taken over the desk by then, I was suffering, so I headed to the monastery."

"That was your only choice?"

"What other choice did I have? There was nowhere to go. Besides, I like it here."

"You took to the monastic life?"

"Oh yes, took to it immediately. Everything's peaceful here, like back in the regiment. Actually the similarities don't end there. Just like in the army, everything's taken care for you: clothes, and shoes, and food, and the authorities look after you, asking only obedience."

"Obedience didn't rub you the wrong way?"

"Why should it? The more obedient a man becomes, the more peacefully he can live. The kind of obedience they ask of me is especially easy: I never have to go to church unless I want to, and mostly I just have to do what they say just like I'm used to. If they say, 'Harness the horses, Father Ishmael' (these days I go by Ishmael), then I harness them; and if they say 'Unharness the horses, Father Ishmael,' then I do that too."

"Pardon us," we said, "but it sounds like you're saying that back at the monastery you got another job working with horses?!"

"From the first day, I've worked as a coachman. My officer's rank doesn't scare them off at the monastery, since, even though I've just recently been tonsured, they treat me as though I were a full-fledged monk like any of them."

"And do you plan on taking your vows soon?"

"I don't plan on taking them at all."

"Why not?"

"I… do not consider myself worthy."

"You mean because of your old sins and trespasses?"

"Well, yyyyes. Besides, what would be the point? I'm perfectly content with the life of obedience I already have. I can live in peace."

"And have you ever told anyone else all that you've just told us?"

"Why, sure. I've told it all more than once. But that's all I can do, without the paperwork to back it up! They don't believe me. They think I've just brought my worldly lies with me into the monastery, that I'm concealing a noble birth from them. None of it matters anymore. I'm getting too old."

The story of the enchanted wanderer, it seemed, was drawing toward its close. All that remained for him to tell us was the tale of how things had worked out at the monastery.

XX

Since our wanderer had reached the closing chapter of his story, the one set at that monastery to which his faith seemed to have predestined him since birth, and since everything there seemed to be working out well for him, we began to have the sense that his life there was charmed, and that Ivan Severyanych had faced down the last of his terrible obstacles. We soon learned that nothing of the kind was true. One of the passengers mentioned that he'd always heard it said that the life of a novice monk is heavily afflicted by the Devil, who torments them day and night, and he asked, "Tell us, please, didn't the Devil try to tempt you in the monastery? I'm told that he's always tempting new monks!"

Ivan Severyanych flashed a peaceful glance at his interlocutor and replied, "Tempt me? Sure, he tempted me. Why, even the Apostle Paul couldn't get away from him: 'There was given me a thorn in my flesh, a messenger of Satan.' If Paul couldn't escape his tortures, what could I possibly hope for, weak and sinful man that I am?"

"What was the suffering he inflicted?"

"Oh, many kinds."

"Along what lines, though?"

"Dirty tricks of all kinds, and at first, before I had over-powered him, he even tried to lead me into temptation."

"And *you* overpowered *him* – the Devil himself?"

"You're surprised? Why, that's a monastery's bread and butter! Still, to be completely frank with you, I might not have succeeded if it hadn't been for the teachings of an old man I met, old as old could be, who had experience and knew a way to resist any temptation the Devil could fling at you. Once I opened up to him about how Grusha was always appearing to me until the air itself seemed to carry her along like a breeze, he spent a while turning it over in his mind and then said, 'It is written by the Apostle James: Oppose the Devil, and he will flee from you. You need but oppose him yourself.' Then he explained what that entailed: 'As soon as you feel that bursting-forth in your heart and the memories of her well up inside you, remember that this is the thorn, the messenger of Satan, and you must be ready to do battle against him. First of all, get down on your knees. A man's knees are his first instrument against the Devil, for as he falls to his knees, his soul flies upward within him. Once you have reached this state of exalta-tion, bow and bow, over and over, with all the strength you have, until you are exhausted. And exhaust yourself also with fasting, even to the point of starvation, for when he sees to what lengths you are willing to be pushed, he usually runs off, fearing that his treachery may backfire and bring its victim directly to Christ, and he thinks to himself, *Better to leave this one alone – perhaps if I don't tempt him that will trip him up faster*. I started doing this, and it worked exactly as he'd said it would."

"Did you have to do it for a long time before the messenger of Satan would leave you alone?"

"I did. It was, in the end, only starvation that drove the nemesis away, since he's afraid of nothing else. At the start I was making thousands of prostrations a day, going four days at a stretch without food or water, until finally he realized that he was no match for me and he softened up, grew weak. Once he saw me tossing my day's rations out the window and picking up my rosary, he knew I wasn't joking around, and as soon as I got back to my knees for more prostrations he ran off. Oh, he's terribly, just terribly afraid of leading men to the consolations of prayer."

"Yes, he… how to put it… he would be, wouldn't he? But even if you overcame him in the end, there must have been a great deal you endured first?"

"Not really. Now that I was oppressing the oppressor, there was nothing too difficult to manage."

"And you're rid of him now entirely?"

"Absolutely."

"He never appears to you anymore?"

"He never comes in the seductive shape of a woman, and if I do see him he's reduced to a pathetic form: squealing just like a little piggy under the slaughterer's knife. I've even stopped torturing him, now I just cross myself and make a single prostration, shuts him right up."

"Well, glory be, that you were able to work this all out so niftily."

"Truly. Though, I'll tell you, having mastered the tricks of the Great Devil, even though it's against the rules, the little ones are always driving me crazy with their mischief."

"So little devils plague you too?"

"They do. They may be insignificant according to their rank, but they'll drive you crazy all the same."

"What sorts of things do they do to you?"

"They're just little kids, and since there's so many of them down in Hell, and they don't have to worry about feeding themselves, they're always asking permission to come up to earth and sow confusion. When they get it they come up and, the more important a man's rank, the more they bedevil him."

"But what do they do, what are some examples? What kind of bedevilment?"

"They'll swap whatever's in your hand for something else when you're not looking, or put something in front of you so that when you walk into it and it breaks, someone else gets mad at you. They get such a kick from this, clapping their hands and running to their elders: 'Look, we've made them confused, give us a penny for it!' You see what I'm saying? They're just… children."

"But what's something specific? What have they done to trip you up?"

"Well, for instance, we had an incident with a Jew who hanged himself by the monastery, and all the novices began muttering that it was Judas himself, that at night he arose and ambled around the monastery grounds, groaning. A lot of us claimed to have seen it. Myself, I wasn't worried in the least – "what," I thought, "will we run out of Jews?" But then one night as I was sleeping in the stable, I saw someone poke his head through the door above the cross-beam and groan. I broke into a prayer – but there he still was, standing there. I crossed myself – he stood there still, and let out another groan. I thought, *what can I do about this. I can't pray for you, because you're a Jew, and, even if you weren't a Jew, I don't have any special dispensation to pray for suicides. Just go! Leave me! Get back into the forest or to the desert.* And I put such a hex over him that he wandered away, and I went back to sleep, but the next night that bastard came back and woke me again with his groaning. The accursed villain just wouldn't let me sleep! I tried to ignore him but I couldn't. "The hell with you, you filth!" I shouted. "Aren't the woods and the church stairs enough breathing room for you, do you have to come thudding to the barn to wake me every night? Since you seem so determined, I'll have to invent another way of keeping you out." So the next morning I drew a large cross on the door in coal, thinking he'd never come back now, but no sooner had I drifted off to sleep than he was back, standing there again, and, if you can believe it, groaning again, too! "Damn you, unworthy prisoner," I yelled, "what's to be done with you!" So he kept me clutching my bedsheets the whole night long, and at first bell I jumped up to rush off and file a complaint with the Rector, when I ran into our bellringer, Brother Diomid, and he said, "You're white as a sheet! What's happened?"

"Oh, this and that, all night I had to put up with such a ruckus, and I'm going to the Rector to complain about it."

But brother Diomid warned me, "I wouldn't waste my time. He's just spent the whole night applying leeches to his nose, which leaves him in an awful mood. But, if you want, I can be of much more help to you than he can."

"It's all completely the same to me. Just help me, I pray – I'll give you my warm old mittens, they'll keep your hands nice and toasty when you're ringing the bells next winter."

"Okay," he said.

I gave him my mittens, and he went up to the belfry and brought down an old church door, painted with an image of the Apostle Peter holding the keys to the Kingdom of Heaven.

"That," he said, "is the most important part: the keys. Put this up against the door, and no one can ever get through."

I was so overcome with gladness that I almost fell at his feet, and right away I thought to myself *why prop this door in front of the other one and keep having to remove it, when I could just hammer it down and make it a permanent barrier?* So that's what I did. I attached the door by sturdy hinges and strengthened it with a big, heavy block of stone on a rope. I did this all quietly during the day, and when night fell I climbed into bed to get some sleep. What do you know – breathing again! I just couldn't believe my ears, it didn't seem possible – but there it was. And not only was it standing there breathing, it was jimmying the door, trying to break it open! The old inside door still had its lock, but I hadn't found time to install one in the outer door – mostly just trusted its sacred nature to keep it safe from intruders. He pushed on that door harder and harder until it was beginning to creak open and I could make out the snout on the front of his disgusting head – and then the weight of the stone pulled it down and slammed the door shut. He leapt away from it, and I could hear him scratching around for a minute, and after a little breather he was at it again, but shoving even harder this time, and again there was just a glance of snout before the door came swinging shut, even louder than before. It must've hit him on the head, too, because he stopped after that and I could go back to sleep, but after a while I was awakened to find that he was at it again and had redoubled his efforts. Now he wasn't just slamming into the door with his horns, he was using them, slowly working the door open with them… and then he was in the room! I threw a sheepskin coat over my head – I was downright terrified by now – but he just grabbed it off me and started licking at my ear. I couldn't take any more of this impudence, so I reached under the bed and grabbed my axe, and I swung as hard as I could at him, and I heard him let out one last moan and collapse where he'd stood. *Well,* I thought, *serves you right.* But just imagine my consternation the next morning, when I looked over and saw no Jew but our monastery cow, which these villainous imps, these minor demons, had switched into his place."

"Was it hurt?"

"I should say so – I killed it with my axe! This raised quite a flap in the monastery, let me tell you."

"It must have been a lot to deal with!"

"Oh, it was. The abbot thought I had imagined the whole thing, probably because I wasn't spending enough time in church, so he blessed me and told me that every evening after I finished with the horses I should come stand next to the screen where the devotional candles are lit. But those little demons hadn't had the last of messing with me, no sir. It was during mass on Shrove Tuesday, while the congregants were taking communion, standing before the abbot and the deacon, and a lady from the church handed me a candle and said, 'Please, Father, put it up there for me.' I went up to the lectern where the ikon of Christ of the Waters was hanging and tried to put down the candle, but my hand bumped another one and knocked it to the floor. As I bent down to pick it up I knocked over two more. Just as I was getting those, well, what do you know – four fell. I shook my head. *Look at those little urchins, up to their usual tricks, knocking the candles out of my hands*, I thought. I crouched to pick them all up, and as I stood up again, I got a terrible knock in the back of the head, and… candles all over the floor. I was incensed. I swept my hand across the platform, knocking down whatever hadn't already fallen. *There's something for their arrogance*, I thought. *I'll knock every candle down before they can get to another*.

"What happened to you after that?"

"They wanted to put me on trial for it, but an old blind monk named Sysoy, a hermit who lives in seclusion from the rest of us, stepped in on my behalf. 'Why should we put him on trial,' he asked, 'when we know it is Satan and his minions who caused this trouble?' So the abbot came to agree with him, and he gave me a blessing and had me confined to a pit in the ground with no need for a trial."

"Were you in the pit long?"

"He just blessed me and sent me down there, never said a word about the length of my sentence. They ended up leaving me down there the whole summer long. Didn't let me out till the first frosts of autumn."

"I imagine that the boredom and torments of the pit must have been worse than out on the steppe?"

"Not at all – how can you even compare them? In the pit I could hear the tolling of the church bells, and sometimes friends would come to visit. They'd come and stand over me and we could have a conversation. Plus, the father treasurer had a millstone lowered for me to grind up some salt for the kitchen. How can you compare it with the steppe or anything else?"

"When they let you out? It must have been because of the frosts, because it had gotten too cold?"

"No, that's not why. It wasn't the cold at all, no, quite a different reason. You see, I had begun to prophesy."

"Prophesy?!"

"Yes, sir. See, while I was down in that pit, I got to pondering, well, just how weak I was in spirit, and how much suffering that had brought me to and how I never could seem to do anything to make it right, and I sent some novice to one of our elder instructors to ask whether he might pray to God to grant me a more suitable nature. And the hermit answered, "Let him pray the way he has been instructed, and then he can await the unawaitable." So that's what I did: for three nights I got down onto those first instruments, my knees, and I keened and prayed with wild fervor and waited to feel perfection take hold in my soul. We had another novice named Gerontiy, amply well-read and a subscriber to lots of newspapers, and one time he gave me a copy of the life of the Reverend Tikhon of Zadonsk to read, and whenever he happened to walking by my pit he'd pull out a newspaper from under his cassock and throw it to me down there. 'Read it,' he'd call down, 'and maybe you'll find something helpful there. At least it'll be some amusement for you, down in your hole.'"

So while I awaited the impossible fulfillment of my prayer, I became a voracious reader. Once I got done with my day's salt-grinding, I'd grab a book, usually the life of the Reverend Tikhon to start with, and I read about how the Holy Mother had come to visit him in his cell, accompanied by the Holy Apostles Peter and Paul. It is written that God's servant Tikhon petitioned the Virgin to prolong peace on earth, and the Apostle Paul thundered back to him with these words: 'When all proclaim and confirm that peace reigns, that is when ruinous calamity shall suddenly befall them.' I thought a lot about the Apostle's words, and at first, frankly, I couldn't make head or tail of them. Then at last I started flipping through all the newspapers, and I read about how here at home and in far-off places, the voices of the world were ceaselessly proclaiming a never-ending and universal peace, and I suddenly understood the saint's words perfectly: 'When all proclaim and confirm that peace reigns, that is when ruinous calamity shall suddenly befall them,' and I became racked with fear for the great Holyrussian people and started praying, and whoever came by for a visit I would admonish through heavy tears, 'Pray, pray that every one of our enemies fall beneath the might of our Tsar, for the day of ruin and hardship approacheth!' The tears that were granted me were granted in such a wondrous abundance! I cried and cried for the motherland. The abbot was informed of all this – they told him, "Our Ishmael in his pit has begun weeping and prophesying war.' The abbot said a blessing for me and had me transferred to the empty shack that stood amid the gardens outside the kitchen, and he had the ikon of Blessed Tranquility brought there, on which the Savior is depicted not with a crown of thorns but as the Lord of Hosts, shaped like an angel with wings graciously folded, hands clutching his breast in resigned acceptance. I was told to make prostrations before the ikon daily until the spirit of prophecy quieted down within me. They locked me away in this hut and I stayed there till spring, praying to Blessed Tranquility, but just as soon as I saw another human being, the spirit would overtake me and I'd start prophesying again. All of this got the abbot to send a doctor over to look at me – had I gone soft in the head? The doctor spent a long time with me there in the cabin, listening to my whole story just as you are now, and afterward he just spat and said, "Well, well, what an old drum you are, brother. They beat and beat you, and it just can't wind you up."

And I said, "What's to be done about it? Indeed, I think it must be so."

The doctor, having taken this all in, reported back to the abbot, "I cannot say what the problem is. Is he just a gentle spirit, is he all shaken up, is he really a prophet? Well, this last possibility," he quickly added, "I'll leave up to you, since prophecies aren't within my specialization. My advice, at any rate, is that you send him off to some faraway place. Perhaps he's been too long standing still."

They cut me loose, and now I'm on a pilgrimage to the tombs of Saint Zosima and Saint Sabbatai in Solovky. I've been all around, but I've never seen them, and I want to prostrate myself there before I die."

"Why do you say 'before you die'? Are you sick, or something?"

"No, I'm not sick. But I want to be ready in case I need to take up arms again."

"Am I to understand that you're talking, again, about going to war?"

"I am."

"So it would seem that this Blessed Tranquility hasn't done you much good!"

"I couldn't tell you. I struggle with all my might to stay silent, but sometimes the spirit overcomes me."

"What does it tell you?"

"All it ever says is: 'Take up arms!'"

"But it couldn't be that you're readying to go back to war?"

"And why couldn't it? Yes, of course, that's exactly what I'm doing: I want so badly to die for my people."

"I don't understand you. You can't go to war in your cowl and cassock!"

"No, sir. When the time comes, I'll take off my cowl and cassock, and don instead my old uniform."

That said, the enchanted wanderer seemed to a feel a stirring of the spirit of prophecy, and he fell into a deep and contemplative silence, which none of us dared interrupt with any further questions. Besides, what else was there to ask him? He had told us the whole sad story of his life with all the candor of a simple soul, and his prophecies for the time being remain in His hands Who conceals His judgments from the wise and the wiser, but Who from time to time reveals them to innocents.

OTHER TITLES IN **THE ART OF THE NOVELLA SERIES**

THE ART OF THE NOVELLA

THIS IS A MELVILLE HOUSE ▣ HYBRIDBOOK

HybridBooks are a union of print and electronic media designed to provide a unique reading experience by offering additional curated material—Illuminations—which expand the world of the book through text and illustrations.

Scan the code or follow the link below to gain access to the Illuminations for *The Enchanted Wanderer* by Nikolai Leskov, which include:

- An essay on Leskov's writing by Leo Tolstoy from *What Men Live By* (1888)
- "The Steel Flea," a short story by Leskov
- Contemporaneous maps depicting the vast territories covered in *The Enchanted Wanderer*
- Rare photographs of Nikolai Leskov
- The story of Anton Chekhov's first meeting with Leskov
- And many more readings and illustrations

Download a QR code reader in your smartphone's app store, or visit
mhpbooks.com/leskov389

THE ART OF THE NOVELLA